THE FORTUNES OF TEXAS

*Follow the lives and loves of a complex family
with a rich history and deep ties
in the Lone Star State*

SECRETS OF FORTUNE'S GOLD RANCH

Welcome to Fortune's Gold Ranch...where the
vistas of Emerald Ridge are as expansive as the
romantic entanglements that beckon its visitors!

A FORTUNE'S SECRET

Drake Fortune doesn't know what possessed
him to invite a down-on-her-luck Annelise
Wellington to stay at his family's sprawling
Emerald Ridge ranch. Yet once the secretly
expectant mom arrives, he can't remember
life without her. Nor does he want to! But
with a ruthless saboteur on the loose and the
appearance of Drake's long-lost twin—literally—
on his doorstep, the unlikely new roommates
don't have any time to fall in love. Or do they?

Dear Reader,

Welcome back to Emerald Ridge and the world of the iconic Fortunes of Texas family!

I'm thrilled to once again be a part of this legendary romance series. This latest Fortunes miniseries is called Secrets of Fortune's Gold Ranch and centers around the Fortune family's luxe guest ranch, complete with a fabulous spa and a working cattle operation. *A Fortune's Secret* is the sixth and final book in this miniseries, and I had the best time writing this story and wrapping up all the ongoing drama! Be sure to pick up the first five books in Secrets of Fortune's Gold Ranch to get the full effect of everything happening in Emerald Ridge, Texas. You can find them at Harlequin.com or any online retailer.

A Fortune's Secret tells the story of Drake Fortune and Annelise Wellington. In the opening chapter, Annelise bumps into Drake and gives him a piece of her mind when he pretends not to know her. But was it really Drake, or a surprise doppelgänger? And that's only the start! Both main characters have a secret. This story and the entire miniseries are full of dramatic twists and turns.

I hope you enjoy your literary trip to this fun Texas town. As always, thank you for reading!

xoxo,

Teri

A FORTUNE'S SECRET

TERI WILSON

THE FORTUNES OF TEXAS

Special thanks and acknowledgment are given to
Teri Wilson for her contribution to
The Fortunes of Texas: Secrets of Fortune's Gold Ranch miniseries.

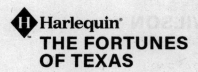

Harlequin®
THE FORTUNES
OF TEXAS

Recycling programs
for this product may
not exist in your area.

ISBN-13: 978-1-335-99683-1

A Fortune's Secret

Harlequin Enterprises ULC
22 Adelaide St. West, 41st Floor
Toronto, Ontario M5H 4E3, Canada
www.Harlequin.com

Printed in Lithuania

MIX
Paper | Supporting
responsible forestry
FSC® C021394

New York Times bestselling author **Teri Wilson** writes heartwarming, feel-good contemporary romance. Three of Teri's books have been adapted into Hallmark Channel movies, including fan-favorite *Unleashing Mr. Darcy*. Teri is a recipient of the prestigious RITA® Award for excellence in romantic fiction and a recent inductee into the San Antonio Women's Hall of Fame. When not writing, Teri enjoys spreading doggy joy with her Cavalier King Charles spaniel Charm, a registered therapy dog.

Books by Teri Wilson

The Fortunes of Texas: Secrets of Fortune's Gold Ranch

A Fortune's Secret

Harlequin Special Edition

Comfort Paws

Dog Days of Summer
Fa-La-La-La Faking It
Bluebonnet Season

Love, Unveiled

Her Man of Honor
Faking a Fairy Tale

Furever Yours

How to Rescue a Family
A Double Dose of Happiness

Montana Mavericks: Six Brides for Six Brothers

The Maverick's Secret Baby

The Fortunes of Texas: Digging for Secrets

Fortune's Lone Star Twins

Visit the Author Profile page
at Harlequin.com for more titles.

To all the Harlequin authors who have been part of the iconic Fortunes of Texas series since its inception in 1996. What an honor it is to walk in your footsteps.

Chapter One

Annelise Wellington would've bet her entire family fortune, Texas mansion included, that whoever had come up with the nonsense about pregnant women glowing had never been dumped by their significant other the instant the word *baby* had come out of her mouth. At three months along, if she was glowing in any way, shape or form, it was a result of her excellent skin care routine. A routine composed of products that Annelise herself had developed, made with waters from the famous hot springs in her hometown of Emerald Ridge, Texas.

AW GlowCare would always be her first baby—the surprise bun currently taking up residence in her oven notwithstanding. Her small business was thriving, thanks to the fact that the fancy spa at Fortune's Gold Ranch was now carrying the entire line of AW Glow-Care products. Taylor Swift recently stayed at the ranch, and according to *Vogue*, she was now using Annelise's GlamGlow moisturizer. Now all the other boutiques in the area had started carrying her beauty products, and her bank account was glowing right along with her dewy, moisturized face.

Unfortunately, that's precisely where Annelise's good luck ended. She could deal with being a single mother, but she wasn't about to let her baby grow up without knowing his or her father. A child needed to feel wanted...loved. Or maybe Annelise was feeling extra sentimental about fatherhood because she was still grieving the loss of her own dad just under a year ago. Either way, she wanted her child to know its father. Also, she was going to throttle Brad.

Just as soon as she found him.

Annelise steered her designer stilettos toward Coffee Connection in downtown Emerald Ridge, because pregnant or not, she wasn't about to give up her girl boss wardrobe until she absolutely had to. Pregnant women could wear heels, just like they could run their own companies. But there was a limit to how long even the most competent multi-tasker could be fueled by indignation alone. She really needed a latte, even though— *sob!*—she was off caffeine because of the baby. But she supposed decaf was better than nothing.

Seriously though, what kind of man breaks up with his girlfriend as soon as he finds out she's pregnant?

Even when she wasn't consciously thinking about Brad or the skid marks he'd left in his wake when he sped off to his new life—in *Paris*, of all places—her befuddlement was always there, lurking in the background. The hurt, too. She asked herself that question at least ten times a day.

Sometimes it even came flying out of her mouth without Annelise even realizing it.

"Excuse me?" the man walking in front of her on the pavement, whose broad, muscular shoulders seemed to span the entire width of the sidewalk, asked as he slowly turned around.

Oh, no. Annelise's bottom lip slipped between her teeth. Had she actually said that out loud…again?

A fresh wave of humiliation coursed through her. She really should've grown accustomed to the prickly sensation of heat in her cheeks by now, as it had been happening pretty much every one of the thirty days since Brad's embarrassingly timed desertion, but she still hated it. She wasn't this pathetic girl who inexplicably had a bare ring finger and a skirt digging into her rapidly expanding waistline.

Except she sort of was.

She squared her shoulders, pasted the beauty queen smile on her face that had once earned her the esteemed title of Miss Emerald Ridge, and tipped her chin up to look the random stranger in the eye and try to pretend she'd been talking about some other pitiful pregnant woman who'd just been dumped.

But, to her utter mortification and maybe just a little bit of fury, he wasn't a random stranger at all.

"You," Annelise spat.

A look of confusion creased his handsome face, because, yes, even men who maintained friendships with awful, terrible human beings could be physically attractive. It happened with alarming frequency, actually.

"Yes, you. Drake Fortune." With a perfectly manicured finger, she poked at his wall of a chest. It was hard as a rock. Truly a wonder that she didn't break a nail. "What do you have to say for your friend, huh?"

Drake and her ex had gone to college together at Texas A&M University in College Station, where Drake had studied ranch management and Brad had studied...

Hmm. Was it weird that Annelise had no idea what the man she'd thought she was going to marry had studied in college? Also, did A&M offer a degree in womanizing? Because that tracked.

"Pardon?" Drake said.

"You heard me." She crossed her arms, feeling protective of her unborn child already, even though—according to the pregnancy books she'd been devouring—at three months along, the baby was no bigger than a plum. "When was the last time you talked to Brad?"

"Who?" The furrow between the man's eyebrows deepened. "Ma'am, are you feeling okay? Can I call somebody for you, or—"

"Save it, Drake." Annelise held up a hand.

She didn't have the time or the inclination for whatever asinine game the jerk was playing right now. Neither did he, she imagined. Shouldn't he be off roping a cow or lifting a barbell or something?

"Look, we don't need to have a heart-to-heart or anything. I get it. You're on *his* side, and that's fine. You're his friend, so he gets you in the breakup. All I want is his contact information." Annelise blew out a breath. She was going to just leave it at that...she really was, but maybe she should tell Drake the truth about what had happened. There was no telling how Brad had spun things.

She'd be doing the guy a favor, actually. The Fortunes were a respectable family. He wouldn't want to tarnish their charmed name by association.

"However, just so you know, your good buddy Brad is lower than the skin on a snake's belly." So much for keeping it classy. "I'm three months pregnant with his baby, and when I surprised him with the big news, he dumped me and told me he was moving to Paris. I haven't heard from him since, and he must've either changed his number or blocked me, because my calls aren't going through."

Drake's stare was so blank that she almost waved a hand in front of his face.

"Did I mention that the aforementioned dumping occurred on our six-month anniversary?" She'd thought he was going to propose. After all, he'd made dinner reservations that night at Captain's restaurant on the top of the Emerald Ridge Hotel.

"It was also my birthday," she added, and a bit of the venom drained from her tone.

She always went a little wobbly when she talked about that part. Her parents had made a huge thing out of her birthday when she was little. When she turned nine, they'd gifted her a horse. A framed photograph from that day—Annelise beaming atop Sugar, a gorgeous palomino, while Daddy held the reins, grinning from ear to ear—held a place of honor on her desk at AW GlowCare. That picture had become her most treasured possession after her father passed away.

But now Annelise's birthday was forever ruined, because she'd surprised Brad with the baby news just after the server at Captain's restaurant delivered a cake to the table—a three-layer beauty from her favorite bakery in Dallas. She'd expected a ring. A proposal had, in fact, been her birthday wish as she'd blown out her candles.

Instead, Brad blurted out the news that he'd just gotten a job transfer and was moving to Paris without her. He'd simply been planning on telling her the day after her birthday...

To be nice.

Before the plumes from the extinguished candles cleared, Annelise's birthday wish had gone up in smoke. Literally.

"So, as I said, I really need Brad's contact information. I don't want to get back together with him. I just want my child to know his or her father." Her eyes filled with tears and she blinked, hard, to keep them at bay. "It's kind of important. Surely you understand."

Drake looked at her like she was completely unhinged. "Um, I think you have me confused with someone else."

Seriously? He'd rather pretend he didn't even know her at all than give up Brad's cell number?

She gave Drake a death glare.

But he just stood there, fully committed to the pretense.

"You know what?" she huffed out. "You're just as bad as my ex. In fact, you might even be *worse*. I'm all for loyalty and everything, but this is beyond comprehension. You and Brad deserve each other, Drake." She regarded him through narrowed eyes. "Drake the Snake. That's what I'm calling you from now on."

With any luck, it would catch on. Doubtful, since he was a Fortune and all. But a girl could dream.

Annelise stormed past him, fury propelling her every step. When had Drake Fortune turned into such a jerk? Granted, she didn't know him all that well, but she knew he was one of Brad's oldest friends. What didn't he understand about her predicament?

She was going to be alone when her baby was born, wasn't she? The only family she had left was her brother, Jax, who lived hundreds of miles away in Galveston, and her semi-wicked stepmother, Courtney.

Courtney isn't all that bad, she told herself. She'd been making a real effort at trying to get close to Annelise since her father's passing a year ago. Courtney had also been doing a great job with the family ranch, overseeing the entire multimillion-dollar cattle and sheep operation all on her own, which left Annelise with plenty of time to focus on her company. Still, sharing the family mansion with Courtney on the ranch's property had been a little awkward. Annelise made a point to stay in her wing, far away from Courtney's bedroom. Privacy wasn't a concern, but sometimes she fantasized about moving out. She just couldn't bring herself to do it. That house and the surrounding ranch property were all she had left of her parents. It had been over two years since her mother lost her battle with cancer, and the one-year anniversary of her father's fatal heart attack was drawing near. If only they were still around to share her pregnancy with her...

Annelise had grown up in Emerald Ridge, but she hadn't been great about keeping in touch with friends. All her time went to AW GlowCare. How could she reach out to people for help or even companionship when she'd missed birthdays, weddings and more than her fair share of girls' nights. Lately, she'd gotten friendlier with Poppy Fortune, Drake's cousin. She always looked forward to chatting with her at the spa at Fortune's Gold Ranch, where Poppy worked as the director. She'd probably love to hear Annelise's baby news. But did Annelise know her well enough to ask her to attend birthing classes with her?

She wished she could convince her brother, Jax, to come back to Emerald Ridge. Her throat grew thick at the thought of having to settle for Courtney as her birthing coach. Surely things weren't that dire. How much lower could she possibly sink? She couldn't even rely on her ex to come back to town for the birth of his child. They'd never be a couple again, for obvious reasons—all of which centered around Brad being a terrible human being. But she was going to have to hold Courtney Wellington's hand while she pushed Brad's baby out, all because Drake refused to turn over her ex's phone number. It was every bit as infuriating as it was devastating.

Hot tears fell down Annelise's cheeks as she spun around to give Drake another piece of her mind, but she was too late. He'd already climbed behind the wheel of a sleek silver SUV parked down the street. Wow, he must've bolted the second she'd brushed past him.

What. A. Jerk.

"I'll have a decaf skinny vanilla latte, please." Annelise smiled at the barista. It wasn't his fault that her life was a hot mess at the moment. "Actually, forget the skinny part. And I'd like it with extra whipped cream."

She was eating and drinking for two now, after all.

"Cow, nut or oat?" the barista asked as he jabbed at the register with his pointer finger.

Annelise blinked. "Pardon?"

"What kind of milk would you like—cow milk, oat milk or almond milk?" he clarified.

"Cow," she said.

Obviously. This was Texas, after all. You couldn't swing a stick around here without hitting a herd of cattle.

She paid the barista and moved to a plush chair by the window while she waited for her coffee. Once seated, she rested a hand on her belly, closed her eyes and took three deep breaths. Getting so worked up while she was pregnant couldn't be good for the baby, and nothing was more important to Annelise than her child. Really, though. She still couldn't believe one of Brad's friends had just pretended not to know her, straight to her face. The indignities just kept piling up, didn't they?

Annelise practiced visualizing a healthy newborn, dressed in a pastel-colored onesie, clutching its perfect, tiny fists. The baby would have her blue eyes, not Brad's beady brown ones. Soft, delicate skin. Maybe she would expand AW GlowCare and add a line of infant care products. She could name them after the baby.

Soothed at last, her eyes fluttered open. The first thing she saw through the window was Drake Fortune smoothly exiting a black Porsche parked at the curb directly in her line of vision, and just like that, her mood plummeted again.

He was back already? And now he was in a fancy sports car instead of the silver SUV he'd been driving before. Annelise frowned. *Weird.* Also, how had he changed clothes so fast? Just a few minutes ago, he'd been wearing jeans and a T-shirt—which, now that she thought about it, seemed very un-Drake-like. Every time she'd seen Drake Fortune in the past, he'd been perfectly polished from the toes of his high-end Lucchese boots to the top of his cowboy hat. Always a Stetson, and always in Drake's signature color—rich charcoal gray.

Her stomach did a little flip at the sight of him, which she blamed on whatever pregnancy hormones were currently coursing through her body, because if there was one person in Emerald Ridge who she absolutely shouldn't find attractive, it was Jake the Snake. She wondered where he might be going, since there were several nice businesses along this stretch of downtown. Then, just as she reminded herself that she didn't care a lick about Drake Fortune or whatever errand he might be running, he steered his fancy cowboy boots straight toward the coffee shop.

Ugh. Annelise did her best to sink into the soft leather of the armchair and disappear. She'd had enough of him today, thank you very much.

Clearly, trying to make herself invisible was a wasted effort, because as soon as Drake crossed the threshold, his eyes found hers.

"Annelise." His mouth curved into an easy smile as he walked straight toward her. "It's been a while. How have you been?"

Well, well, well. Look who'd just gotten over his case of temporary amnesia.

"We just ran into each other a few minutes ago on the street," she said crisply.

"I don't think so. I just pulled up a second ago." Drake hitched a thumb over his shoulder in the direction of his Porsche, and his smile broadened. "Besides,

I'm sure I'd remember if I'd just bumped into you. It's nice to see you again."

What is happening?

Surely she hadn't just accosted a total stranger by mistake. No possible way. The other Drake had looked exactly like the Drake standing in front of her. Same close-cropped blond hair. Same dreamy blue eyes. Same muscular build, as if he spent his spare time on his cattle ranch carrying bales of hay on his broad back or hauling young calves around instead of sitting behind a desk in a luxurious corner office, which was the more likely scenario for a Fortune.

Even so, an image of Drake bottle-feeding a fawn-colored newborn calf suddenly popped in her head, and she went a little swoony—proving once and for all that those pregnancy hormones were a very real thing.

She swallowed hard and redirected her gaze away from the biceps straining the seams of his Western shirt and back toward his face. "Truly, Drake. You must have a doppelgänger running around somewhere. I just had a conversation with a man who looked exactly like you. In fact, he could've been your identical twin, except for the clothes."

Not to mention the annoyingly aloof personality...

"Actually, I mistook him for you." Annelise bit her lip. Wow, she'd really given the non-Drake a piece of her mind, hadn't she? "I called him Drake the Snake for pretending not to know who I was."

The corner of Drake's mouth twitched, like he was trying not to laugh. "Drake the Snake, huh?"

"It just slipped out. I was upset." Annelise scrunched

her face. Understatement of the century. She couldn't believe she'd let the fake Drake make her *cry*.

"Clearly." The amusement in his features softened and turned into something else…something that made her throat close up tight. "For the record, I would never pretend not to know you, Annelise. You're not an easy person to forget."

Her heart turned over in her chest, because he said it like it was a good thing. Not like she was the unhinged ex-girlfriend of his college buddy who'd just chased his dead ringer down on the sidewalk and yelled in his face.

"I know we haven't seen each other in a while, but I heard that you and Brad aren't together anymore." Drake shifted his weight from one booted foot to the other. "And I know he broke up with you on your birth-day. I'm really sorry. That's just…"

He shook his head, as if at a loss for words. Speech-less—as he should've been, instead of weirdly detached, like the other Drake.

"I know, right?" Annelise forced a laugh as she blurted out the rest. "If you think that's bad, I'd just told him I was pregnant with his baby."

Surely Drake already knew. He and Brad were friends. He was probably just being polite and tiptoeing around that little nugget of information so she wouldn't feel uncomfortable.

But the instant she mentioned the baby, she realized she'd miscalculated. Drake's mouth dropped open. Then his gaze darted to her midsection and quickly shifted back to her face. He'd obviously had no idea she was pregnant.

"Oh, Annelise," he said, and the gentleness in his tone was too much to take.

She didn't want Drake Fortune's pity. Anything but that.

"Surprise," she said with forced cheer. She spread her fingers into jazz hands and wiggled her fingertips.

Now who's pretending?

She sighed and dropped her hands into her lap. "I told the doppelgänger, too. You're the only three people who know—you, Brad and fake Drake."

The barista finally called her name, but Annelise couldn't seem to move, despite the fact that she clearly needed a latte. She was normally so polite, and overnight she seemed to have lost any semblance of a filter. She was also seeing double, and not one of her pregnancy books had listed that as a hallmark of the first trimester.

Embarrassment pinned her in place as her face burned with the heat of a thousand Texas summers. What was wrong with her all of a sudden?

More importantly, who *was* the guy she'd seen earlier, and why did he look so much like the very real, very charming Drake Fortune?

Chapter Two

Drake watched Annelise's pretty heart-shaped face turn three shades of red as he tried to process what she'd just told him.

She was pregnant. Moreover, he was the only person privy to this sensitive information, save for the baby's father and a random man she'd yelled at on the sidewalk. Also, the rando apparently bore a striking resemblance to Drake himself.

Never in his life had he taken part in such a bizarre conversation. He knew this with absolute certainty, because the fact that she was so convinced he had a doppelgänger was the least concerning part.

First things first. His friend Brad was an unbelievable cad. He'd dumped his pregnant girlfriend on her birthday, mere moments after she'd told him about the baby. Drake could barely wrap his head around such behavior, even knowing what he did about Brad. He'd never been a completely stand-up guy back at A&M, where they'd become friends mainly because they'd been randomly assigned to the same dorm suite their freshman year. But they'd been kids back then. Drake only saw the guys from the dorm a few times a year for poker night. The conversation never strayed far from Aggie football (or Aggie baseball or Aggie basketball), so it was hard to get a read on anyone's personal life. But they were supposed to be grown-ups now. Drake had certainly matured since his twenties, and he'd assumed his buds from college had too.

Apparently not.

You're too good for him. You always were. That's what Drake wanted to say to Annelise, but he wasn't sure it was entirely appropriate. She seemed a bit fragile at the moment—understandably so—and he didn't want her to think he was trying to hit on her when she was at her most vulnerable. Clearly what she needed most right now was a friend.

"Let me grab your coffee for you." Drake tipped his head toward the counter, where her latte sat waiting. "I'll get some treats for us, too, if you don't mind me joining you for a bit? I'd love to stay and chat for a while, if you'd like some company."

A jolt of…something…skittered through him, as if he'd just asked her out on a date and was nervously awaiting her answer—which was most definitely *not* the case.

"Um…" Annelise hesitated.

"I hear the lemon loaf is fantastic," he said, although for the life of him, he couldn't figure out why he was trying to talk her into letting him stay. "And you *are* eating for two now."

He winked.

One of her graceful hands fluttered to her belly, and

she smiled at him, acknowledging their secret. "Well, when you put it that way, how can I refuse?"

Drake delivered Annelise's latte to her and then placed their order. Minutes later, he was seated across from her in the cozy nook by the window. Sunlight filtered through the tempered glass, creating a gold halo around her long brown hair. Dark bangs skimmed her lashes, making her eyes seem impossibly big and blue.

Yep, definitely out of Brad's league in every possible way.

"So, why haven't you told anyone else about the baby?" he asked quietly as he placed her slice of cake in front of her. She was going to have a hard time keeping it secret if she glowed like this all the time. Annelise had always been beautiful, but pregnancy clearly agreed with her.

"I don't know." A smile blossomed on her lips. "I'm excited. I can't wait to be a mother, but it's only the first trimester and I guess I'm afraid to jinx things. Plus with my relationship status the way it is, I feel a bit…"

"Vulnerable?" he prompted.

She'd been planning on saying she felt awkward. Possibly even embarrassed. But she liked the way he phrased it much better. "Yes, vulnerable is the perfect word. I know my friends wouldn't judge me, but I haven't seen much of them in a while. I keep thinking I'll tell people after I get my life figured out. Meanwhile, no one knows."

"Other than me." He grinned as he poked at his slice of lemon loaf with his fork. "And Drake the Snake."

He was teasing her, because he wanted to keep things light and friendly. But the fact that she was going through this alone didn't sit well with him. She needed a support system.

"Right, other than you two." She laughed a little, and then her expression turned wistful. "I just started my business a year ago, and since then, I've pretty much spent all my time working, which didn't give me much time for a social life. Brad used to complain about that, actually."

Drake's jaw tensed. The next time one of the guys organized poker night, his answer was going to be a firm pass. "You've built an incredible brand. Don't ever let anyone feel guilty about that. You should be proud."

He'd been seeing AW GlowCare all over town for months now. Fortune's Gold Guest Ranch and Spa, the luxe property located on the same sprawling acreage s his family's cattle operation, had also started carrying it. From what Drake heard, Annelise's skin care line was flying off the shelves.

"Thanks for saying that," she said as she picked at her lemon loaf.

"I mean it. Starting your own business from scratch is hard. It usually takes years for a new product line to get off the ground, and you're already in *Vogue*."

Annelise's eyes widened.

"What?" Drake asked as he took a gulp of coffee.

"I guess I just never pegged you for a *Vogue* reader." She looked him up and down. "Although that might explain the fit of your Western wear. You've always been a stylish man, Drake Fortune."

"My sister showed me the article." He arched a brow. "But by all means, tell me more about how attractive I am."

"I said *stylish*," she corrected him, but her cheeks went pink all the same.

Were they flirting? It sure felt like it.

Drake cleared his throat and steered the conversation back to safer ground. "Just so you know, I haven't talked to Brad in months. I heard about the breakup through the grapevine."

He winced. Despite its close proximity to Dallas and a reputation as one of the wealthiest resort towns in the state, Emerald Ridge was still that—just a small Texas town. News traveled fast.

"I guess that means you don't know how to get in touch with him now that he's living in Paris." Annelise pushed her plate away. Great. He'd just killed her appetite.

Drake felt himself frown. "Afraid not. I'm sorry."

She sighed, and her gaze dropped to her lap. "It's okay. I'll find someone else to be my birthing coach. I've still got six months to go."

"I can't really see Brad being great at that, honestly. We're not close, but I know he's not the most reliable guy." Drake nudged the tip of her stiletto with his boot to get her to look up at him again. "But everyone has their good points, and so did he. I'm sure your baby will only inherit those from him. None of the bad ones."

"None of the bad ones," she echoed, and then her smile was back, and Drake felt like he'd finally said something remotely useful. "That's enough Brad talk. Tell me what's going on with you and your family. Is there any word about the mastermind behind the recent thefts and sabotage on the wealthy ranches in the area?

And ooh, tell me how Baby Joey is doing. Are y'all any closer to figuring out who his real mother might be?"

Of course she'd wanted to hear about Baby Joey. The infant who'd been left on the front steps of the main house at his family's ranch just a few months ago was all anyone in town could talk about.

Drake's parents, Hayden and Darla, shared the main house with his dad's cousin Garth and Garth's wife, Shelley. Drake had grown up in the grand mansion, as had his siblings, Micah and Vivienne, and his cousins, Poppy, Rafe and Shane. Now the younger generation of Fortunes all had their own stately homes at Fortune's Gold Ranch, gifted to each of them on their twenty-first birthdays.

On the night the baby appeared on the doorstep, Drake's cousin Poppy had been having dinner with his Aunt Shelley, along with their neighbor, Courtney Wellington. Since Courtney was Annelise's stepmother and they shared the big mansion on the Wellington Ranch, she probably had more than a casual interest in the baby. Plus, she was pregnant. She had babies on the brain.

But the abandoned infant was just the tip of the iceberg as far as Fortune family drama went lately. After Poppy answered a knock at the door during dinner, she'd found the baby boy nestled inside a blue baby carrier and wrapped in a onesie embroidered with the name *Joey*. A note had been tucked into the carrier that said, *This baby is a Fortune. Please care for him since I can't.* The family, along with law enforcement, had been searching for the baby's mother ever since, along with trying to determine the identity of Joey's father and if, in fact, he was a Fortune. Drake and all the other Fortune men had submitted to DNA testing back in January, but the county crime lab lost the results. The recent thefts and vandalism at local ranches had the crime lab working overtime, and apparently, balls were being dropped left and right.

They'd redone the DNA tests, though, and found out that the baby wasn't a Fortune after all, which only complicated things further. A mysterious text indicating that Joey was the son of Garth Fortune had obviously been a lie. Then a young woman named Jennifer Johnson had shown up in town, claimed Joey as hers and tried to extort half a million dollars from the Fortunes for "pain and suffering" in what appeared to be a thinly veiled attempt to *sell the baby*. That had proven to be a ruse, as well.

"I'm afraid we're still in the dark about a lot of things." Drake shook his head. "Even though we've proven that Jennifer Johnson is *not* Joey's mother, we still believe she's got to know who the real birth mom is."

"How are you so sure?"

"Well, she managed to initially fool the crime lab with a fake sample for the DNA test. Clearly she got it from someone," Drake muttered.

Annelise leaned closer and lowered her voice. "And she won't just be up front and give your family the real mother's name?"

"Nope. She's still trying to get five hundred thousand dollars out of us, this time to fork over a name." The audacity was unbelievable. Drake saw red every time he thought about it, especially because his cousin Poppy was growing more attached to the little tyke by the day. Joey had been just a day old when he'd been abandoned on the Fortunes' doorstep. Poppy was the only mother he'd ever known, and she'd cared for him with her whole heart and soul. He worried what might happen if she had to relinquish custody. This mystery would surely get solved...eventually. *Then what?* "We're obviously not giving in to her demands. The woman's already proven she can't be trusted. But we're stringing her along to try and buy some time while we keep searching for the truth. If she skips town, we'll be all the way back to where we started."

"What a mess," Annelise whispered.

"The *messiest*." Drake blew out a breath. "Meanwhile, the crime lab is piled high with fingerprint testing and evidence analysis from the vandalized ranches, and there are still no credible leads. My family is working night and day on all of this, as are the police."

"It's so kind of Poppy and Leo to take care of Joey in the meantime. I bet they'll miss that little guy something awful if he's returned to his birth parents." Annelise curved a gentle hand over her midsection. She was already attached enough to her own baby that she couldn't imagine having to say goodbye. It was written all over her lovely face.

Drake's throat grew thick. He liked Annelise. He didn't want her to go through her entire pregnancy alone. And a baby needed all the love it could get.

He ought to know. Drake had been adopted by his mom and dad as a baby. He'd only been a newborn when Hayden and Darla Fortune had added him to their family, and Drake didn't really know anything about his birth parents. But sometimes he wondered what might've happened to him if he hadn't been so lucky.

Annelise would obviously be a wonderful mother, but he couldn't help feeling a twinge of empathy for her baby. If Brad was already actively trying to avoid her and had changed his number, there was no chance he planned on doing right by his child.

"Poppy and Leo would be happy to adopt Baby Joey, given the chance," Drake said. For a while there, when everyone thought Jennifer Johnson was truly Joey's mother, that had been the plan. Poppy had been devastated when she'd learned the truth, but that hadn't stopped her from doting on the child like he was her own.

Annelise wasn't the only one with babies on the brain, apparently.

Drake pushed lingering thoughts of cribs, rattles and fatherhood out of his mind and smiled. "As for the ranch sabotage, I'm at a loss. My sister, Vivienne, and her fiancé, Jonathan, are convinced the mastermind behind it all is another rancher trying to snuff out the competition. But only two ranches in the area haven't been affected, and both the families behind those operations are people the Fortunes have known for years. *Good* people." He sighed. "So much about this doesn't make sense, and there doesn't seem to be an end in sight. Didn't you have more trouble over at your family's place a while back?"

Annelise nodded. "We sure did. The first time we got hit, the criminals cut a hole in one of our fences big enough to let four head of cattle escape. This most recent time, we lost five. Luckily, Courtney managed to get them all back."

That certainly ruled out the Wellingtons. Annelise's family ranch had been one of the first ones targeted back in February, and they were still in the crosshairs.

Not that Drake had ever really suspected them to begin with, even though the Fortunes and the Wellingtons had something of a long-standing feud between them. Supposedly, a full century ago, a groom from the Fortune family left a Wellington bride at the altar, breaking her heart and publicly humiliating her. In the rocky aftermath, the Fortunes presented an aged bottle of wine from the nearby Leonetti Vineyards to the Wellingtons as an apology. Unfortunately, the rare bottle, valued at over $1,000 even back then, had somehow gotten skunked. The rancid gift had only escalated the feud, but over time, it had become an old Texas story. More of a legend than anything else. Courtney Wellington was a frequent guest at the main house at Fortune's Gold Ranch. As for Annelise…

Drake couldn't imagine her doing something so nefarious. She was a hardworking businesswoman who'd been born into wealth and privilege—just like he had—but she wanted to create something special, new and all her own, completely from scratch. And she was succeeding.

Drake couldn't help but admire her.

Between her work at AW GlowCare and having her heart broken just after discovering she was expecting, Annelise clearly had a lot on her plate. He couldn't exactly picture her sneaking around cutting fences and stealing saddles. The idea was almost laughable.

"The truth will come out eventually. It always does," he said. He just hoped both mysteries would be solved before anyone else got hurt. It was bad enough that cattle and horses had been lost. But Joey was a helpless baby. He deserved better than being dumped on someone's doorstep like a piece of abandoned trash.

Just thinking about it made Drake's gut churn.

That unwanted child could've been me.

"Oh, no. I've got to go!" Annelise jumped out of her chair, and suddenly, her midsection was just inches from his face.

He blinked, mesmerized for a beat by the sight of her hand pressed so protectively against her belly. His gaze drifted over her nails, painted a delicate pink, like the color a mom might choose for her baby girl's nursery room walls. Then his eyes landed on her bare ring finger, staring him right in the face.

Drake cleared his throat and stood. "Is everything okay?"

"Yes. I'm sorry." She held up a hand—the one without an engagement ring. "I didn't mean to startle you. I just realized what time it is."

"We've been chatting quite a while, it seems," Drake said, removing his Stetson and holding it in front of him like he'd been taught to do as a gesture of respect back in his preteen cotillion lessons at the country club. "I didn't mean to keep you."

"You didn't." She shook her head and hiked her designer handbag further up on her shoulder. "I mean, I enjoyed it, actually."

"Me too," he murmured, and there it was again—that jolt of awareness that he'd felt before and vowed to ignore.

His grip on the brim of his Stetson tightened, fingertips digging into the pressed felt.

"I have a prenatal appointment with my obstetrician this morning. If I don't hurry, I'll be late." Annelise tucked a stray lock of her dark hair behind her ear.

"Of course. Don't let me keep you. I'll get our cups and plates. You go take care of your little one." He winked. "And don't worry, your secret is safe with me."

She pulled a face. "Your doppelgänger might be another story."

"Yeah, I can't make any promises on behalf of that guy." He chuckled. "But if I happen to stumble across him, I'll make sure he keeps his obviously handsome mouth shut."

Annelise laughed, and the sound soothed him, like country church bells on a Sunday morning.

He liked making her smile, and he realized that he wished he could do more for her... Crazy as it sounded, he wished they could stay right there for the rest of the day, just the two of them in their cozy little nook while the rest of the world went on without them.

"Thank you, Drake," she said softly, and her expression went bittersweet. "I really mean it. For everything."

"Anytime," he replied, once again cursing Brad Nichols.

He'd hurt her, and as tempting as it might be to consider himself a stand-in—even for just this past hour or so—Drake was nothing of the sort. He and Annelise had shared coffee and a dessert. Brad and Annelise shared *a baby*.

Drake wasn't sure why that thought made his chest clench the way it did.

"Goodbye," Annelise said with a flutter of her fingertips, and Drake had the nonsensical urge to offer to accompany her to the doctor's appointment.

He swallowed the idea down before it accidentally came flying out of his mouth. "Goodbye, Annelise. Take care, and let me know if you need anything. I really mean that."

"I will." She nodded.

And then she was gone, leaving Drake with that strange ache behind his sternum that told him just how badly he wanted to believe her.

Chapter Three

Drake tossed his Stetson onto the leather passenger seat and took his place behind the wheel of his black Porsche 911 coupe. The June heat was stifling, so he cranked up the AC and moved seamlessly into downtown traffic as he did his best to push all thoughts of Annelise Wellington out of his head.

He had enough to worry about with the area ranches under threat and the Baby Joey mystery still hanging over the heads of the entire Fortune family. Which meant he didn't need to be heaping more onto his plate than absolutely necessary.

Still, when his cell phone vibrated with an incoming text, he snatched it from the middle console without missing a beat in case it was Annelise. Maybe she'd decided she needed a hand to hold at her doctor's appointment after all. Anxiety snaked its way up Drake's spine as he scanned the text. Surely she hadn't gotten bad news. He hadn't stayed long at the coffee shop after she left, but given the size of Emerald Ridge, she'd probably already had time to arrive and get settled at her appointment.

The text wasn't from the pretty brunette, though. It was from his brother, Micah. Before Drake had a chance to read it, another text popped up, and then another. The notifications were coming so fast and furious that Drake finally pulled his car over to the side of the road.

He flicked through the texts as quickly as he could. Every message appeared to be from one of his siblings and cousins back at the ranch, and the tone grew progressively more urgent with each missive.

Micah: Where are you?

Shane: Hey, man. You might want to head home.

Poppy: How fast can you get to the ranch?

Rafe: You need to come home. There's a...situation.

Micah: WHERE ARE YOU?

Vivienne: I'm calling you in two seconds. Please pick up. It's urgent.

Drake's pulse began to gallop fast and hard. What was going on?

His phone rang before he could respond to a single message, and as promised, his sister Vivienne's name flashed on the screen.

His panic spiked as he accepted the call. "Viv?"

"Yeah, it's me." She took a breath so deep that Drake could hear her shaky inhale. *This can't be good.* "Something's happened at the ranch."

"So I gathered. My phone just started blowing up." He gripped the phone tighter as a livestock trailer rumbled past his car. A longhorn swiveled its massive head toward Drake and stared impassively at him.

"You need to get to the ranch as fast as you can. Come straight to the main house," Vivienne said.

"What's this about?" His mind reeled with possibilities. Had someone had an accident? One of his parents, maybe? Uncle Garth or Aunt Shelley?

"I can't explain over the phone. Just get here pronto," she insisted, and then *click.*

The line went dead.

Drake shifted the Porsche into Drive and maneuvered back onto the road. Wide-open fields dotted with freshly rolled bales of hay and herds of grazing cattle passed by in a blur. By the time the engine rumbled onto the ranch's main drive, his hands ached from clenching the steering wheel. The large mansion stood, stately and sprawling beyond the wrought-iron gates. It had always looked more like a castle to Drake than a ranch house, but for him and the rest of the Fortunes, it was also home. He slammed the car into Park and took the steps leading up to the grand double doors two at a time.

"Hello?" he called as he stepped inside.

He could hear voices coming from the living room, so he headed that way, boots clicking on the smooth marble floor of the entryway. But then his parents entered the foyer to greet him, stone-faced. Drake's gut churned as his gaze flitted from his father to his mother, but then someone stepped out from behind them…

And Drake couldn't believe what he was seeing.

"I'm sure there's a perfectly reasonable explanation, but please know that your father and I are just as stunned by this as you are," his mom said calmly, but her voice barely registered.

The man standing beside his parents looked exactly like him. Not just a little bit, but *identical*. Other than the way the man was dressed, it was like looking at his own reflection in a mirror.

"The doppelgänger," Drake said under his breath.

Annelise had tried to tell him, but he hadn't really taken her seriously. He'd assumed she'd simply mistaken him for someone else who might've borne a passing resemblance to him. But this...

This was more than a slightly similar appearance. This was a lookalike. A dead ringer. No wonder his entire family had been trying to track him down.

Somehow, someway, Drake Fortune had a long-lost identical twin.

He stared for a beat as he tried to collect his thoughts. His lookalike blinked back at him, forehead creased in confusion with what was surely an identical expression to the one on Drake's face.

Drake's mom, Darla, wrung her hands, while his dad, Hayden, stood beside her, the set of his jaw as hard as granite. Someone needed to say something, but who? And what? Everyone in the foyer had been rendered speechless.

"Pardon me for being so blunt," Drake said to the doppelgänger once he finally found his voice. "But who the hell are you?"

The man wiped his palms on his jeans before walking forward and extending a hand. "I'm Cameron Waite."

"Drake Fortune," he said as he shook the man's hand.

The name sounded vaguely familiar, but Drake couldn't quite place it. He was a tad preoccupied by the sight of a living, breathing carbon copy of himself.

Cameron blew out a breath. "I have to say, this isn't at all what I expected when I got the invitation in the mail a while back. I'm adopted. I'm guessing you are too?"

"I am, but you mentioned an invitation…" Drake felt himself frown. He couldn't think straight. He might even need to sit down. "What invitation?"

"Mr. Waite received a Gift of Fortune invitation," Darla said and waved a hand, motioning for him to show Drake the letter he'd received.

"It's right here." Cameron pulled a cream-colored envelope from his pocket and handed it over.

Cameron Waite was printed on the outside of the envelope in typewritten script, and as Drake ran the pad of this thumb over the lettering, he realized why the name had sounded so familiar.

Last month, he'd heard one of the front desk clerks at the ranch's guest house mention that a Cameron Waite had recently called because he'd received a Gift of Fortune invitation for a weeklong complimentary stay. The Gift of Fortune Initiative had been started by Drake himself, along with his cousin Rafe, as a goodwill outreach to people in need of an emotionally healing place to stay. Over the course of the past few months, they'd hosted guests who were struggling to overcome broken hearts, mental health challenges, marriage difficulties and more.

The idea had been Drake's brainchild, inspired by his adoption as a newborn. He knew nothing at all about his birth parents, but he'd often wondered about them and what circumstances had led to his mother having to give up her child. He appreciated the life he had now and wanted to help others the same way he'd been given a helping hand when he'd been at his most vulnerable.

Just like Annelise.

Drake swallowed. He could think about her later. Right now he needed to figure out where Cameron Waite had come from and how he'd ended up with a Gift of Fortune invitation, because as soon as the front desk had mentioned the reservation, it had raised a red flag in Drake's mind. He'd never extended an invitation to anyone named Cameron Waite, and if memory served, neither had Rafe.

Sure enough, once he'd consulted his cousin, Rafe confirmed that he hadn't issued an invite for anyone by that name either. And it wasn't as if Gift of Fortune invitations were easy to come by. Shortly after they started the project, Rafe set up an online form for folks to nominate recipients who might benefit from a complimentary stay. The process was rigorous, and decisions weren't made lightly. Other family members chipped in and helped read the applications—even Hayden, who hadn't exactly been on board at first.

Drake's dad liked to call him a bleeding heart. The criticism had started way back when Drake was a kid and he wanted to save every runt and orphaned animal he came across. Ranch life could be hard at times, even on an opulent, three-thousand-acre spread like Fortune's Gold Ranch. The family had long employed hired help to deal with the day-to-day nitty-gritty work of running the cattle operation, but somehow Drake had always seemed to find out when a horse pulled up lame or a newborn calf refused to nurse or was slow learning to stand. He'd spent more hours than he could count sneaking out of his room at night to sit cross-legged on a pile of straw and bottle-feed animals in the darkened barn. His father found him out on more than one occasion, no doubt thanks to ranch hands hesitant to hide anything from the big boss.

He still remembered the first time his dad loomed over him with crossed arms and a Stetson pulled down low over his eyes while the weak calf in Drake's lap slurped at a bottle. Neither of them said a word at first. The only sound in the quiet stall was the steady smacking noise of the calf tugging at the rubber nipple.

Finally, Hayden spoke. "They're not pets, son. They're livestock, and we have people to do this for us."

Drake's gaze never strayed from the newborn calf. "Everyone deserves a fair shot at life, though. And I wanted to help."

His parents had always been open and honest about his adoption, while at the same time making sure he felt like he was as much part of the family as his brothers and sisters were. Drake was a Fortune, through and through. But he hadn't been *born* a Fortune, and he never forgot that his life could've gone a completely different way.

Memories swirled through his mind as he ran his thumb over the gold embossed invitation. If neither he nor Rafe invited Cameron Waite to Fortune's Gold Ranch, then who had? And why did the embossing look just a bit off, as if it had been done with different equipment than what they used here at the ranch?

Someone had known that Drake apparently had a secret twin.

But why...*why*...had they brought him here to Emerald Ridge? Was this supposed to be some kind of ambush? Because it sure felt like one.

He handed the invitation back to Cameron. "This appears to be genuine, but I'm not sure who sent it. It must've been mailed without the knowledge of anyone on the Gift of Fortune team."

How was that possible, though?

"I have no idea who sent it or why they picked me. Although now that I've seen you, it doesn't seem at all accidental." Two lines formed between the man's eyebrows. If his body language and the shock written all over his face were any indication, he'd been caught off guard by all of this too. Drake wasn't the only one being manipulated. "Originally, coming here sounded like a great opportunity, but I've only been in town twenty minutes or so, and people keep mistaking me for someone else."

He looked up at Drake, shook his head and laughed a little under his breath. "Now I know why."

It sounded like Annelise's encounter with Cameron had only been the tip of the iceberg.

Drake waved a hand back and forth between them. "I suppose this explains a lot about your rocky welcome to Emerald Ridge."

"It does, but it also raises plenty of questions. Someone clearly wanted us to meet," Cameron said.

Drake didn't have the first clue who would've done this. He turned toward his parents, who were still gaping at the sight of Drake and his surprise lookalike. "Mom, Dad? Do you have any idea what's going on here?"

Hayden shook his head. "No idea, but the adoption agency has a lot of explaining to do."

His mom rested gentle fingertips on Drake's forearm. "They never told us you had an identical twin, honey. If they had, of course we would've adopted both of you."

"Absolutely." Hayden nodded.

"Cameron, are you close with your adoptive family?" Darla asked.

"*Was* close," Cameron corrected her, switching to past tense. "Yes, ma'am. Both my parents were wonderful people, but they've passed on. I grew up in a house that looked a lot like this one, actually."

He glanced around the wide foyer and smiled, and Darla's rigid posture seemed to relax a little bit. If Drake knew his mother, the guilt at leaving a baby behind was eating away at her, even though she hadn't known Cameron existed. At least it sounded like he'd been raised in a good home.

"And you've lived in Texas all this time?" Hayden asked.

Cameron nodded. "In Dallas."

"To think you've been only an hour away." Darla's hand fluttered to her throat.

"Mom, why don't you go sit down? This has obviously been a huge shock to everyone." Drake glanced at his dad, who was nodding behind his wife's back as he rested a hand on her shoulder, ready to guide her to the kitchen, no doubt for a glass of the sweet tea she loved so much. "I can get Cameron settled in the Gift of Fortune cabin. Where's everyone else, though? My phone was blowing up earlier, so I get the feeling I'm the last of the cousins to know I'm a twin."

Darla waved a hand. "We sent them all home once you said you were on your way. We figured you and Cameron might need some time to yourselves before adding more Fortunes to the mix."

"Good idea," Drake said. He loved his siblings and cousins, but just the thought of multiplying the current drama by five was enough to give him a migraine of epic proportions.

"Go show Cameron around. We'll be here if either of you has any questions, although I'm afraid we don't know much more than you do at this point. I'll dig up the adoption papers from the family safe." Hayden clapped Cameron on the back. "It's a pleasure to meet you. Enjoy your stay here at the Gold Ranch."

Drake was glad his parents had treated Cameron with kindness instead of skepticism. While it was certainly odd that he'd turned up out of the blue, Drake had a gut feeling that someone else was pulling the strings behind the scenes of the mysterious Gift of Fortune invitation. Too many unusual things had been going on in Emerald Ridge lately. They had to be connected...

He just needed to figure out how.

But first, he wanted to talk to Cameron and get to know him. He had a *twin*. How had he never had an inkling that there was someone walking around who looked exactly like him?

"What would you like to see first?" Drake asked as they stepped outside and onto the mansion's wide covered porch. "I can show you around the spa, although that's really my cousins' domain. And of course I'd be happy to give you a tour of the cattle operation. We're cutting hay on the back acre right now."

The sweet smell of freshly baled hay in high summer was always nostalgic for Drake. One of the things he loved best about being a rancher was the steady rhythm the life afforded. Ranching had seasons, just like the weather—calving season, branding time, turning the cattle out—and he found comfort in the predictability of it, year after year. From the cattle to the churned earth on which they trod, ranching was rich with tradition. He'd always loved feeling like he was part of something that was timeless, even if he wasn't as hands-on as he'd been when he was a teenager riding on the back of a tractor in late June during the first cutting.

Cameron's gaze swept the horizon, and Drake felt a swell of pride. It felt good to share this place he loved so much with one of his blood relatives, at long last. "You know, I think I just want to head on over to the guest cabin, if you don't mind. All day long, people have been looking at me, thinking I'm you. I could use some more time to wrap my head around things before we walk around together and completely freak people out."

A laugh rumbled from deep in Drake's gut. "I completely understand. But once you get settled and the news has had some time to sink in, I'd like to try and figure out more about our adoption. I've never searched for any information on my—sorry, *our*—birth parents, but given the circumstances, I'm beginning to think that might be a good idea."

There had to be a way all these puzzle pieces fit together, and if Drake and his secret twin had something to do with all the strange things going on in Emerald

Ridge, he was willing to do whatever it took to dig up the truth. Even if it meant unearthing the most painful part of his past.

There was a good reason he'd never wanted to know about his birth parents. People didn't give up their children unless they felt like they had to. Whatever the story might be, it was sure to be a sad one. Perhaps having a newly found brother along for the ride might take away a bit of the sting.

"Finding out more about our birth family seems like a really good idea." Cam nodded. "I have so many questions, and I'm sure you do too."

Drake slid his gaze toward his twin and wondered if he'd ever get used to looking into eyes that mirrored his own. "Any chance you'd be up for figuring out the answers together?"

Cameron's familiar face split into an easy grin, and for the first time since they'd laid eyes on each other, he seemed to relax a bit. "Absolutely. I'd like that a lot."

Chapter Four

Annelise glanced around the waiting room at the doctor's office, and her heart gave a pang. The chairs were filled with couples. Maybe it was only her imagination playing tricks on her, but it seemed as if they were all gazing lovingly into each other's eyes, like she'd stepped into a picture-perfect advertisement for prenatal vitamins or something.

Just to her right, a man ran his hand tenderly over his significant other's pregnant belly. *Get a room*, she thought and rolled her eyes. But it only took a modicum of self-awareness to realize she wasn't annoyed at the sweet display of affection.

She was envious.

Hold your head up high. Women have babies on their own all the time, she reminded herself as she squared her shoulders and headed for the check-in desk. They just didn't do it here, in this office, apparently. From the looks of things, she was the only expectant mother in the building who'd shown up unaccompanied for her appointment.

Obstetricians should have a special day for single

expectant moms. Like ladies' night at a bar, only with pickles, ice cream and foot massages instead of half-price alcoholic beverages. Maybe Annelise should jot that idea down for her doctor's suggestion box. Or maybe she was completely losing it.

Probably the latter.

"Hi, I'm Annelise Wellington, here for my appointment," she said.

The woman in pink scrubs glanced up from her computer screen and handed her a clipboard. "Great. Please fill out these registration forms and bring them back with a copy of your insurance card." Her eyes darted to the empty space beside Annelise. "Did anyone come along with you for your appointment?"

Sure. My baby's father couldn't wait to support me through this special time, only he's invisible. That's why you can't see him.

"No, it's just me," Annelise said, and weirdly, her thoughts skipped directly from Brad to Drake Fortune.

He'd been so kind to her earlier—kind enough that she was accidentally thinking about how different her life would be right now if he'd been the father of her baby and not Brad. Which was completely absurd, because they barely knew each other. Drake was no doubt busy going about his day without giving her a second thought.

"Are you okay?"

Annelise blinked. The receptionist was still talking to her, and she'd completely zoned out while her mind snagged on a certain pair of blue eyes and the way they'd glittered beneath the brim of a gray Stetson.

Drake had insisted she should call if she needed anything. She'd told him she would, even though she had no intention of following through on that promise. It was nice to think about, though, especially at a time like this.

"Sorry. I got distracted for a second." Annelise smiled at the woman behind the desk and tightened her grip on the clipboard. "I'm fine."

Totally, one hundred percent A-OK.

Maybe if she kept repeating it to herself, she'd actually start believing it.

Drake spent the next hour or so in the Gift of Fortune guest cabin with Cameron, talking about their lives and childhoods, doing their best to catch each other up on a lifetime of separate memories. Even though they'd been adopted by two completely different families, their lives had followed eerily similar paths.

Like the Fortunes, Cameron's adopted family, the Waites, were wealthy landowners with long-standing ties to Texas. He'd grown up in Highland Park, an iconic old-money neighborhood in Dallas, attended private schools, and now ran the family business, just like Drake. The Waites were bankers instead of ranchers. After Cameron's parents passed away, he took his father's place as CEO. During college, he'd attended the University of Texas at Austin, the rival school to Drake's alma mater, Texas A&M, which explained why they'd never crossed paths before.

It was going to take a lot longer than an afternoon to truly get to know his brother, but Drake liked Cameron. He seemed to be a great guy. As much as he was looking forward to deepening their relationship, he felt emotionally drained when he pulled the Porsche into the circular drive of the stately home where he lived alone on the Gold Ranch property, then killed the engine. This day had been full of surprises and overstimulation. He sat in the quiet car for few minutes, reveling in the solitude, until the late June heat became unbearable.

Once inside, he removed his Stetson, tossed his keys onto the console table in the foyer, and checked his phone as he made his way to the den. He'd had his cell on silent the entire time he'd been with Cameron, and even though it seemed unlikely, he was hoping that Annelise might've reached out to tell him about her doctor's appointment.

She hadn't. Instead, he had another slew of missed calls and texts from his cousins and siblings, wanting answers about his dead ringer. From what Drake could tell, they'd all had individual run-ins with Cameron around town earlier in the day. Now they wanted the full scoop, even though Drake still only had very little information to share.

He opened the family group chat and fired off a message.

Sorry, guys. I need some time to digest everything. Bottom line: I've got a twin I never knew about. I'll update you all when I know more, but turning off my phone for now.

As soon as he hit Send, Drake made good on his promise and shut down his phone. Then he drummed his fingers on the arm of the sofa for less than half a second before boredom set in.

He'd never been one for sitting still. When he'd been

a kid, he'd constantly been labeled a wiggle worm by his teachers. Even today, his office had a standing desk because sitting too long made him restless. This morning with Annelise had been the first time in, well, *ever* that being still for a while had him feeling peaceful. Grounded. Content.

There was something about her that made him want to stay in the moment instead of thinking about a million different things all at once. Drake had assumed it was her pregnancy. A baby just had a way of making the less important things fall away...of bringing a sense of clarity and purpose to everyday life. But deep down, he knew the explanation wasn't quite that simple.

He was attracted to Annelise. And yes, that probably violated every version of the Bro Code in existence, but after what Brad had done to her, Drake didn't much care. It wasn't as if he was ever going to act on his feelings, anyway. That wasn't the kind of support Annelise needed right now. He wanted to help restore her faith in people, not make it worse.

Drake stood, grabbed his keys and got back in his car. Driving always helped when he was feeling unsettled. Texas and its wide-open spaces had a way of helping him get out of his head and reminding him that his problems were small in the great big scheme of things. He loved the rolling landscape of the hill country and the flat, endless horizon of the plains all the same.

But when the Porsche roared to life and Fortune's Gold Ranch receded into his rearview mirror, Drake didn't head to either of those places. Instead, he found himself heading straight for the Wellington Ranch...

For Annelise.

* * *

"Drake Fortune?" Courtney Wellington raised her chin as her gaze flitted from Drake's eyes to his steel-gray Stetson and back again. "My goodness, this is quite a surprise."

The summer sun beat down on Drake's back, penetrating the starched fabric of his Western yoke shirt as he stood on the front porch of the Wellington mansion. It wasn't completely unheard-of for him to show up here. They were neighbors, after all. But since both ranches were composed of vast amounts of acreage, the properties were relatively far apart.

Still, Courtney was looking at him like he was visiting royalty or something, which was…weird. That was Courtney Wellington, though. Drake had always found her to be a bit on the dramatic side. The edges of her razor-sharp blond bob ended just at the corners of her mouth, painted with a creamy coral lipstick. At just under forty, she was closer to her stepdaughter's age than she'd been to Annelise's father. She'd always been nice enough to the Fortunes, but if the *Real Housewives* franchise ever came to Emerald Ridge, Drake was betting on her to snag a starring role.

"Hello, Courtney," he said. "Is Annelise home?"

Courtney's eyes—which already looked a little too big for her face, given the extreme length of her faux eyelashes—widened. "You're here for Annelise? Isn't that interesting…"

"We bumped into each other in town this morning," Drake said by way of explanation. Not that it was any of Courtney's business, necessarily.

"Come on in and get out of the heat, then," the

woman said, waving him inside. "I'm not sure if she's home or not. This house is just soooo large, you know."

Drake shook his head. If she was trying to impress him, she was wasting her breath.

"I'll text her for you," Courtney said, tapping her long nails on the screen of her cell phone.

"Thank you. I appreciate that." Drake cleared his throat.

"Oh, look. There she is now." Courtney nodded toward the curved staircase with decorative iron railing that spilled out onto the foyer's slick marble floor.

"Drake?" Annelise floated down the steps, mouth curving into a bashful smile as her gaze found his. "What are you doing here?"

He had to stop himself from rushing to help her down the stairs in case she accidentally tripped and hurt the baby.

What had gotten into him? Annelise had grown up in the house. She'd probably gone up and down this staircase thousands, if not tens of thousands, of times.

He shouldn't have come here. That much was already clear. He was overstepping, and he couldn't seem to stop. His whole world had been thrown for a loop with the arrival of Cameron Waite, and now all his emotions were simmering just beneath the surface like a tender bruise.

"Annelise." He held up a hand, consciously aware of her stepmom watching him like a hawk. "Hi."

"Well—" Courtney said, grabbing a tangerine-orange Birkin bag from a polished oak table by the front door "—as fascinating as this unexpected development is, I've got to run. I was just heading out for a bit."

"The Fortunes live right next door, Courtney. I'm sure Drake is just being neighborly. There's no 'development,'" Annelise insisted.

Duly noted. Drake's smile stiffened.

"Or maybe he's here because there's news about the recent sabotage." Courtney turned questioning eyes on him. "Has your family heard anything about the identity of the person who paid the thief to steal the saddles from your ranch?"

Last month, in a stroke of luck, one of the vandals had finally been caught red-handed on Fortune property. He'd claimed to law enforcement that he'd been paid to steal saddles and let horses free but refused to give any details about who'd hired him. Which meant they were no closer to figuring out who was responsible than they'd been before.

Drake sighed. "No, I'm afraid not. The thief still isn't talking, but I know the police are working hard on the case."

"I should hope so. Those saboteurs cut another section of our fence a few weeks ago." A crease formed between Courtney's eyebrows.

Worry spiked through Drake. As far as he knew, Annelise and her stepmother occupied the big house all by themselves. Sure, there were plenty of ranch hands who lived on the property, too. But he didn't like the idea of them being in the mansion all alone while the thieves were at large—especially Annelise. So far, no one had been physically hurt. But the attacks were becoming more frequent and more brazen. The last thing she needed to worry about during her pregnancy was her physical safety.

"I'm off." Courtney hiked her handbag farther up her forearm until it dangled from the crook of her elbow. "Drake, we'd sure appreciate it if you kept your ears open, and let us know if you hear anything, okay?"

"Of course." He nodded.

She breezed out the big double doors, leaving Drake and Annelise alone together, and prickles of awareness coursed through him. Along with a few nerves. How was he supposed to explain appearing at her door out of the blue?

"I just—" he started.

At the same time, Annelise began talking, too. "I can't believe—"

They both abruptly closed their mouths, gazes colliding for a beat. Then they laughed.

"You first." Drake tipped his hat.

"Okay." A pink flush settled in her cheeks. "I was going to say that I can't believe you're here. Would you like to sit down? I don't have any lemon loaf on hand, but I make a mean root beer float."

"Root beer float?" Drake chuckled. "That's a mighty specific beverage offering."

She shrugged one slender shoulder. "Pregnancy cravings. It's my favorite thing at the moment."

"Sounds great, then." He grinned.

Annelise led him through the massive living room, which boasted thick crown molding decorated with gold leaf, toward a commercial-sized kitchen, where she began scooping vanilla-bean-flavored ice cream into two frosty mugs she pulled from the Sub-Zero freezer.

"Can I do anything to help?" Drake asked as he settled onto a barstool opposite the kitchen counter from her.

"Not at all. You're my guest, and besides, I've got this down to an art by now." She glanced up from the carton of ice cream. "Thank you for not mentioning the baby in front of Courtney, by the way."

"I told you that your secret was safe with me. I'm guessing you still haven't confided in her?" Drake had thought maybe she'd be ready to share the big news after her doctor's appointment. Not so, apparently.

She shook her head as she opened the stainless steel refrigerator and removed two glass bottles of root beer. "You're still the only one. Obviously, I'm going to have to tell her, eventually. She's going to notice when I start showing."

Annelise poured root beer over the mugs of ice cream until both were filled to the rim with a foamy head. She slid one of the frosted glasses toward him. "Or when she realizes how much ice cream we're going through. Whichever comes first."

Drake held up his mug for a toast. "To the baby. And to keeping secrets."

Annelise tapped her glass against his. "Cheers."

"Speaking of secrets…" Drake dipped a spoon into his float. "…I've got a doozy for you. I just found out I have a secret twin."

"What?!" She set her mug down with a clunk and gaped at him. A little ice cream mustache lined her upper lip.

Drake itched to kiss it right off her face. Instead, he handed her a napkin and said, "You've got a little something right there."

He couldn't help but smile as he gestured toward the ice cream on her face. Maybe coming here hadn't been such a bad idea, after all. They'd been so open and honest with each other earlier, and that same connection was still there—a pull that he couldn't quite resist. Giving in to it made him feel better already, despite the fact that he was no longer altogether sure who he was.

You're a Fortune, he reminded himself. *Always have been, always will be.*

Drake still very much believed that, but the arrival of Cameron Waite changed things somewhat. How could it not?

"The doppelgänger you mentioned earlier? He's real. And you were right—the guy looks exactly like me," Drake said. Then he gave her a brief rundown of everything that had transpired since he'd last seen her, including the plan he and Cameron had made to try and find out more about their birth parents.

"I can't believe you have an identical twin you never knew about." Annelise winced. "And I *yelled* at him."

She groaned, and before he realized what he was doing, Drake reached across the counter to rest his hand on hers. To his immense relief, she didn't pull away. "It was an honest mistake. If it makes you feel any better, you're not the only person in Emerald Ridge who bumped into Cameron and mistook him for me."

"Did anyone else call him Drake the Snake?" She bit her lush bottom lip, and Drake's grip on her fingertips tightened of its own accord.

He cleared his throat and withdrew his hand before he did something utterly stupid like give in to temptation and lean across the counter to kiss her. He could practically taste the lingering chill of root beer on her lips.

Drake blinked. Hard. "I'm sure he won't hold it

against you. Cameron was as surprised as I was to find out he's a twin."

"Maybe you can apologize for me?" Annelise scrunched her face as she wrapped her hands around her mug. If she'd noticed his gaze flitting repeatedly to her mouth, she didn't let it show.

Good. He still had a shot at keeping this interaction firmly in the friend zone, where it belonged.

"I'm happy to, although I'm sure no apology is necessary," he said.

"So, is that why you stopped by? To tell me about your secret twin?" She toyed with the spoon propped inside her nearly empty mug, swirling it in slow circles.

"Yes and no." He offered her a smile that he hope showed that he cared how she was doing. No matter how terribly his friend had behaved, her baby deserved to feel loved and wanted. So did Annelise. "I also wanted to see how your doctor's appointment went. I figured you might not have anyone else to talk to about it."

"You're right about that." She laughed under her breath. "It was fine, though. Great, actually. The doctor said we can do an ultrasound next month, and I'll be able to find out if I'm having a boy or a girl."

Drake's heart gave a little leap. Did that idiot Brad have any clue what he was missing? "That's wonderful. Do you have a preference?"

She rested a hand on her flat stomach. "No, I just want him or her to be healthy. But it will be fun to find out. At least I'll know what color to paint the nursery."

Her gaze drifted upward, toward the top floors of the mansion, and her smile faltered a bit.

"Hey, what's wrong?" he asked, knowing it was a

loaded question. So much about this situation was complicated. Drake could picture Annelise having one of the fun, over-the-top gender reveal parties that Vivienne and Poppy talked about, but doubted she'd get the chance if she was trying to keep her pregnancy a secret.

"Sorry." She blew out a breath. "It's just hard to imagine living here with a baby in my parents' home, knowing they never got the chance to meet their first grandchild."

"I'm sure that's rough. You and Courtney aren't close, I'm guessing?"

"No." Annelise shivered. "If you want to know the truth, sometimes she makes me uncomfortable. That's why I haven't told her about the pregnancy yet. My brother, Jax, won't have a thing to do with Courtney. She's the entire reason he won't come back to Emerald Ridge."

Drake's teeth clenched until he felt a muscle tick in his jaw. "I'm not sure I like the thought of you living here if you don't feel safe."

"It's not like that. It's just…" She sighed and shook her head. "I can't really put my finger on it. She's really been making an effort lately. I can tell she wants us to be closer, and I have her to thank for AW Glow-Care products being used and sold in the Fortune's Gold Ranch and Spa. That's been incredible for my business. You have no idea…"

"But?" he prompted and raised his eyebrows.

"But she still rubs me the wrong way. She has ever since she and my dad started dating so soon after my mother passed away. The one-year anniversary of losing my dad is coming up soon, which makes her all the harder to take. I miss the way things used to be before Courtney was even in the picture. Does that make any sense at all, or is it just pregnancy hormones? Maybe I'm being irrational."

"You don't sound irrational in the slightest." He gave her chin a gentle nudge with the tips of his fingers, urging her to meet his gaze. "You sound like someone who misses her family."

Her eyes grew shiny, two infinite pools of blue. A man could lose himself in eyes like those...if he gave in and let himself, which Drake wasn't going to do. If anything, this conversation was solidifying the fact that Annelise needed a friend.

"I think the best thing you can do right now is to trust your instincts," he said quietly.

"Right, because my instincts have such a great track record." She rolled her eyes, no doubt thinking about Brad.

For the hundredth time today, Drake wanted to pummel that loser.

Instead, he simply stood, gathered the empty root beer mugs and carried them to the sink. He didn't want Annelise waiting on him when things should so obviously be the other way around. So long as she stayed here with Courtney Wellington, that would never be the case.

"There *is* one other thing you could do." Drake turned to face her, leaning against the kitchen sink with his arms crossed. He needed her to hear what he was about to suggest and know that he meant it with the utmost sincerity.

She tilted her head. "What's that?"

Drake felt a smile tug at the corner of his mouth. This entire day had been filled with surprises, and it was about to take another dizzying turn.

"Move in with me."

Chapter Five

Annelise waited for Drake to laugh, but despite the smile dancing on his lips, he did nothing of the sort. He simply arched an eyebrow at her like the gesture was the final punctuation mark on the absurd sentence he'd just uttered.

"You're serious, aren't you?" She pressed a hand to her stomach to try and stop the sudden fluttering she was sure had zero to do with the baby she was carrying and everything to do with the fully grown man standing in front of her.

"As a heart attack," he said without missing a beat.

Annelise didn't know what to say. Had he lost his mind? She couldn't *move in* with him. Until this morning, they'd barely known each other.

But there was no denying that they'd clicked. She enjoyed spending time with him. In fact, when she'd come down the stairs earlier and spotted him standing at the threshold, her heart had done a full somersault. Just like back when she'd been a teenager on prom night, floating down the curved staircase in her puffy tulle gown while her date waited at the bottom, holding her pink wrist corsage.

He wasn't an awkward teen boy, though. He was Drake Fortune—an old college friend of her ex. And she was pregnant with said ex's child. Nothing about this scenario was romantic in the slightest.

"Is that the real reason you came over here? Have you been hiding that offer away in your back pocket this entire time?" Not that it mattered. Annelise was simply trying to buy some time while she figured out what to say.

She couldn't accept his offer, obviously. But for some reason, her mouth didn't quite remember how to form the word *no*.

"I just thought of it, actually," Drake admitted gruffly. "But come on, you have to admit it's the perfect plan. If you stayed with me, you wouldn't have to worry about Courtney. You'd have someone nearby to confide in—someone who already knows about the baby. Someone who's dealing with their own family drama and might also like the idea of having a friend around."

Friends.

Annelise liked the sound of that, even if someplace deep down, she felt a tiny stab of disappointment. Which was *crazy*. She had no right to expect more. Recently heartbroken pregnant women didn't just go around dating, and they *especially* didn't date their ex's friends.

"You almost make it sound like I would be doing you a favor," she murmured, even though it was so clearly the other way around.

"You would. I'm going to worry about you now that

I know Courtney makes you feel uncomfortable. Not to mention the fact that there are still criminals at large somewhere that seem to be targeting the Wellington Ranch." Drake pinned his blue eyes on hers. "If we're staying under the same roof, at least I'll be able to sleep at night knowing you're safe and content," he said.

Content...how long had it been since Annelise had truly felt that way? She couldn't even remember.

Drake glanced around the spacious kitchen and clicked his tongue. "I can't promise that you'd be living in the lap of luxury like you are out here. My parents, aunt and uncle live in the main house at our ranch. I've got a decent-sized place out there, though, with its own guest suite that would be all yours." A slow smile came to his lips. "And the baby's too, of course. You're welcome to stay as long as you like."

He'd well and truly lost the plot. Now he wanted her to stay with him even after the baby was born? He couldn't possibly know what he was signing on for.

"Babies cry, Drake. At all hours of the day and night," Annelise reminded him.

He arched a brow. "I'm aware. My family just had a one-day-old infant dropped on the doorstep, remember?"

"You don't really want this." She shook her head, because the only thing worse than turning him down would be saying yes and then having him instantly regret the offer.

"I'm not Brad, Annelise," he said softly, cutting straight to the chase in a way that made her eyes sting with unshed tears. "You can trust me, I promise. It would be my pleasure to stand in for my former friend."

Not friend, but *former* friend. Annelise felt her mouth twitch into a grin, but what exactly was he suggesting?

A tear slipped down her cheek—a telltale sign of just how much his generous offer meant to her...and how desperately she suddenly wanted to say yes. She couldn't trust herself, though. Not after the epic disaster on her birthday. How was she supposed to forget what a terrible judge of character she'd been in her past relationship?

Drake held up his hands and walked toward her as tentatively as if she was a spooked horse, which seemed about right, because her heart was galloping a mile a minute. "I only meant standing in for him in a platonic way. Let me be there for you, Annelise. I can help make sure you take your prenatal vitamins, buy giant stuffed pandas, whatever you need."

Lord help her, she was going to do it. She'd been so sad lately, thinking about how different everything had been since the loss of her dad. More than anything, she just didn't want to feel so alone anymore. Navigating pregnancy in secret all by herself was exhausting. Her heart had taken such a beating, and now Drake was stepping up in a way the supposed love of her life had never even considered.

Wild horses couldn't have dragged the word *no* from her lips.

"Aren't you forgetting something?" she said, tipping her chin up to meet his gaze. He was standing so close now—close enough for her to breathe in his rich scent of clean soap, saddle oil and fresh-cut hay. It made her head spin.

His forehead crinkled beneath the brim of his Stetson. "What's that?"

"We're going to need ice cream and root beer. Lots of it."

"Done." He winked, and it seemed to float right through her on butterfly wings.

He was wonderful—the complete and total opposite of Brad—and his kindness was a godsend, right when she needed it most. Someday, he'd probably make a wonderful husband and father. To someone else, not her. Because they were just friends. He'd said so himself, and that was just fine with Annelise.

It was really too bad she'd never truly trust a man again as long as she lived, Drake Fortune very much included, because this man was a real catch.

The following day, Annelise packed her things for her stay at Drake's house. It was hard to know how much to bring since she didn't really have any idea how long she might be there.

Common sense said to limit herself to whatever she could pack into her three-piece luggage set. Showing up at Fortune's Gold Ranch with a U-Haul would certainly turn heads, and that was the last thing she wanted. Already, she had no idea how he planned on explaining his new living situation to his family. Annelise wasn't even sure what *she* was going to say to Courtney, although it might be days before her stepmother noticed she was gone. It wasn't as if the two of them hung out on any regular basis.

Annelise would've loved to have the sort of stepparent who enjoyed girls' nights in fuzzy slippers, baking cookies and binge-watching comfort shows like *Gilmore Girls*. She couldn't imagine Courtney with a spatula in her hand, though. Plus, Courtney had been off sugar and carbs for months, which probably had a lot to do with why Annelise felt like they had nothing whatsoever in common.

They rarely even ate dinner together (again, the carb thing), which was perfectly fine. Annelise could simply disappear and Courtney would be none the wiser, which was great. She'd acted ridiculous when Drake had shown up yesterday, like she was beside herself at the idea of her stepdaughter dating a Fortune.

They *weren't* dating. Annelise just didn't know how to explain why she was living there without mentioning the baby. The new living arrangement didn't make sense otherwise. It barely made sense as it was.

"What's all this?"

Annelise nearly jumped out of her skin at the sound of Courtney's voice. Her gaze flew toward the entrance to her bedroom. Sure enough, there was her stepmother, standing in the doorway, openly staring at the half-packed collection of suitcases spread on top of her bed.

"Courtney." Annelise swallowed. "You startled me."

"Going somewhere?" the older woman asked, without bothering to explain why she'd suddenly turned up in Annelise's wing of the mansion.

"Yes, actually." She finished folding one of her favorite pencil skirts into a neat square and tucked it in place in her largest bag. The skirt had a matching fitted blazer with a ruffled peplum at the hem. The days of wearing that particular ensemble were probably numbered, given the timeline of her pregnancy, but she'd yet to shop for maternity clothes.

She had so much to do before the baby came, and now that she was moving into Drake's house, she was starting to feel excited about her pregnancy to-do list instead of overwhelmed.

"I'm going to go stay with a friend for a while," she said. It was the honest truth. She wasn't sure why it felt like a tiny white lie. "I've been sad lately in this gigantic house without Daddy. I'm sure with the anniversary coming up, you feel the same way."

"Anniversary?" Courtney's face went blank. Clearly she had no idea what Annelise was referring to.

Unbelievable.

Annelise forced a smile. She couldn't wait to get out of here. "The one-year anniversary of my father's death. It's in eleven days."

"Oh, that. Of course." Courtney nodded and pressed a hand to her heart as her expression immediately turned sympathetic, but Annelise wasn't sure if she was buying it. "You poor thing. I'm sure this is a terribly difficult time for you."

Her throat clogged. This was all just too much. Everything in the house reminded her of her father, but Courtney's presence tainted it somehow. She couldn't wait to wake up in the morning someplace new, without all the lingering baggage, even though she felt a tiny bit guilty about leaving this big house behind when it was all she had left of her parents.

It's not forever, she reminded herself, swallowing around the lump in her throat. *It's just temporary.*

She and her baby couldn't very well live with Drake

forever. Eventually, he'd want to get on with his life. This was simply a time of respite—a much needed break from her complicated life.

But what did it say about her sad family dynamics that she was already dreading her return?

"This is a difficult time for me too, obviously, so I understand how much you need to get away." Courtney glanced around the room, gaze traveling from suitcase to suitcase. Her eyes narrowed slightly when they turned back toward Annelise. "How long did you say you'd be gone, again?"

She closed her bag and yanked the zipper shut. The sharp hissing sound it made cut through the loaded silence like a knife.

"I didn't."

Drake swung his front door open with one hand while balancing a white cardboard cake box from Emerald Ridge Bakery in the other.

"Welcome home." He grinned at Annelise and flipped the box's lid open, revealing a round cake, decorated with swags of pale pink icing and cherries sitting atop swirls of whipped cream. "And happy birthday!"

Her eyes lit up, and she laughed. "But my birthday was weeks ago."

"Yes, I know." Drake held the door open wide, even though she'd shown up with a surprisingly small amount of baggage. Three suitcases sat at her feet, from small to medium to large. That was it. Her car was plainly visible, parked behind his Porsche in the circular drive, and it didn't seem to contain any boxes or additional

luggage. "But as I recall, you didn't have a proper celebration. I thought that needed rectifying."

He'd offered to help her pack up and move, but she'd
insisted on doing it herself because she didn't want
Courtney Wellington to find out where she'd gone. So
Drake had spent the morning preparing for her arrival.
There was a new set of root beer mugs chilling in the
freezer already, and a giant stuffed panda propped on
the king-sized bed in her suite. He'd meant it when he'd
said he wanted to stand in for the baby's father, inas-
much as that was possible.

Drake hated that she associated him with the jerk
who'd hurt her. After their initial encounter at Coffee Connection downtown, he'd felt moved to do something—
anything—to help take away a little bit of that pain.

Then Cameron had shown up.

Somehow, the combination of being the only person to know about Annelise's pregnancy, paired with
the shocking realization that he had a twin, had forced
Drake to think about his childhood in a new light.
Hayden and Darla Fortune had never hidden the fact
that he was adopted. He'd grown up hearing the story
of how they'd chosen him to be part of their family, and
it had always made him feel special...*wanted*.

Then, in third grade, he'd done an oral report at
school about being adopted, and he'd finally seen the
flip side of the coin. Kids being kids, some of them
teased him about being a "fake Fortune." They com-
pared him to the stray dog the ranch hands at Fortune's
Gold Ranch had recently rescued, and instead of feeling
chosen, Drake had gone home from school that day with
a whole new awareness of what adoption actually meant.

His birth parents had given him up. As a *baby*. The Fortunes might have wanted him, but his own flesh and blood hadn't.

Drake was a grown-up now and knew better than to let a bully from his childhood affect his mental health. He hadn't thought about that day in elementary school in ages. But looking at Cameron brought it all back— the hurt, the confusion, the endless wondering...

Drake would move heaven and earth to make sure that Annelise's child never felt that way. Babies deserved to feel love and cherished, and he knew without a doubt that Annelise would shower her child with adoration. He could tell how much she loved her baby just by the way she glowed. But one day, that baby would learn the truth about his or her birth father, and the world might suddenly look like a different place. Harsher... meaner perhaps. It grieved Drake to think about it, and he wanted to fix it before it ever happened.

But of course none of that explained the birthday cake. Or the root beer mugs. Or the giant panda waiting for her in her room. He'd done those things for Annelise, not her baby, and Drake knew better than to think too long on his motivation. Some things were better left unexamined.

"I can't believe you got me a birthday cake." Annelise cupped her hands over her mouth and shook her head, but she couldn't hide the smile in her eyes. It made his chest feel like it was filled with sunshiny warmth.

Easy there, partner.

Drake cleared his throat.

"Here, why don't you take the cake to the kitchen while I bring your bags inside?" He handed her the bakery box and jerked his head toward the open living area just beyond the foyer. "It's that way."

"Sounds great, but hurry. I'm not making any promises there will be a crumb of cake left if you drag your feet." She gave him a playful grin as she breezed past him, stilettos clicking in the tiled entryway.

It took superhuman effort not to follow the sound of those glossy heels and stare at her curves, perfectly accentuated in one of the slim skirts Annelise favored. Somehow, he managed. But jeez, she had to be one of the most glamorous pregnant women he'd ever set eyes on.

And now she was living in his home. What could possibly go wrong?

Everything, if he didn't watch his step.

"This cake is *diviiiiine*," Annelise said, drawing out the last syllable while her eyes drifted closed.

Drake had barely set her suitcases down when she'd suggested skipping candles and plates. Locating the silverware drawer clearly hadn't been a problem, because she'd handed him a fork and said that diving right in "*Gilmore Girls*–style"—whatever that meant—would be the culmination of every birthday wish she'd ever had.

Now they stood on opposite sides of the kitchen counter with the rapidly disappearing cake between them, and Drake couldn't help but think that living with a woman was infinitely better than he'd ever imagined...

Not that he'd ever come close to making that kind of commitment before. Sure, he'd dated. Lots of women, in fact. His relationships just always seemed to fizzle out before they got serious.

"Happy birthday," he said, clinking his fork against hers. A chunk of strawberry sponge fell from the tines of his utensil.

Annelise laughed. "Thank you. You have no idea how much I needed this. Have I mentioned that Courtney doesn't eat sugar?"

"No, but I'm hardly surprised. That sounds like the number one character trait of an evil stepmother. Disney should take note." Drake speared his fork into the cake again.

Annelise grinned. "Now you sound like my brother."

"Are you and Jax close?" Drake asked.

"Not as close as I'd like. It's hard with him living so far away. We've barely seen each other since Courtney came into the picture. I keep telling him he hasn't really given her a chance." Her expression turned serious. "But now that I'm here instead of back at the Wellington mansion, I think I'm only just beginning to realize how uncomfortable living with her makes me feel. I've been here less than an hour, and it already feels like home."

Their eyes met...held.

Heat curled down Drake's spine in the most nonplatonic way imaginable. Then Annelise's breath hitched, and all the longing in the world seemed to be contained in that one small gasp. Drake could sense it bottled up in her chest, just like it was in his.

Maybe she felt it, too—this bone-deep pull he was finding it harder and harder to ignore. Maybe her feelings about Courtney and cake didn't have anything at all to do with why she felt so at home here. Maybe telling her how beautiful she looked right now, with her shoes kicked off, her dark hair tumbling down her back and that beatific baby glow about her, wouldn't be the worst thing Drake could say...

"Annelise, I—" he started.

But then her fork slipped from her fingertips and landed on the counter with a clatter, and the moment passed.

Annelise blinked as if waking up from a daze. She backed away from the cake...from *him*...and smoothed down the front of her silk black-and-white polka-dot blouse with its voluminous bow tied at the neck like she was straightening her armor.

"Maybe I should get my things unpacked. I'm sure you have better things to do than babysit a pregnant lady." Her gaze flitted toward her matching set of luggage as if she'd rather have been looking at anything other than him.

Super. He'd managed to make her feel ill at ease in record time. Which was the very opposite of his intentions. Either he'd misread the chemistry between them, or she was gun-shy after Brad's treatment of her. Given that she'd just been eyeing him in the same way she looked at the cake, Drake's money was on the latter.

Which meant from now on, he'd have to double his efforts to be on his best behavior. "I'll show you to your suite."

He grabbed the handles of her wheeled luggage and gave her a brief tour of the house on the way to her bedroom with its en suite bathroom and accompanying study, which he secretly hoped she'd want to turn into a nursery. As a self-professed "fixer," he hated the thought of her raising the baby alone.

Annelise smiled and nodded and said all the right

polite things as he showed her around, but the easy-going camaraderie between them was gone. She seemed guarded, even when she gasped at the sight of the floor-to-ceiling windows that spanned an entire wall of the den.

"This view is *incredible*," she said, gaze spanning the horizon.

"I chose the house closest to the working part of the ranch so I could keep an eye on the cattle." Drake nodded toward the herd grazing in the distance, tails swishing and heads lowered toward the emerald-green grass.

Dappled sunlight filtered through the oak trees, and the sky seemed to stretch on forever, endless and blue, as it only could in the great state of Texas. All six of the homes the Fortune cousins occupied were situated about a quarter mile from each other in loop dotted with clusters of live oaks and Ashe juniper trees to afford maximum privacy.

"I like to sit right here when I drink my morning coffee." Drake nodded toward the pair of worn leather armchairs he'd snagged from the library in the main house when his mother and aunt were in the middle of redecorating.

He liked the nostalgia of older pieces—furniture that told a story. Drake loved ranching for the same sort of reasons. In a romantic sense, ranching was a pastoral return to the past, but he also relished the timelessness of it. Generations from now, the Fortunes would still be here, working the same land. Maybe Drake would have a child someday who followed in his footsteps.

His gaze strayed toward Annelise's hand resting serenely on her midsection, and his throat tightened.

"You mean you like to sit here with your morning coffee on the days you don't go in town to Coffee Connection," she teased, referencing their accidental meeting the day before.

He grinned. "Touché."

Her eyes went soft again, and Drake breathed a sigh of relief. He wanted this arrangement to work for her, regardless of the attraction between them. They were two grown adults. Surely they could keep their hands off each other for the sake of her baby.

"The only thing you haven't shown me yet is my room." She glanced past him toward the hallway that led to the bedrooms.

He hadn't pointed out his room either, but Drake figured skipping that part of the tour might be for the best.

"Come on, then. I'll lead the way."

He rolled her bags into the guest suite and flipped on the light. Annelise bit her lip and walked inside, casting an appreciative glance at the butter-yellow walls and the delicate floral bedding he'd recently bought to replace the brown plaid that had been there before. Then she noticed the giant stuffed panda on the bed and the antique rocking chair by the window, and her hands fluttered to her heart.

"Oh, Drake. This is all too much—the cake, the panda, the rocker." She sniffed, and Drake suddenly didn't know what to do with his arms, because he wasn't sure wrapping her up in a hug would be the wisest choice.

"I'm glad you're here. All I want is for you and the baby to feel like this is your home," he said.

The rocker had been another piece he'd liberated from the main house. He doubted Mom and Aunt Shelley would notice, since he'd found it tucked away in the attic. Good thing, or Poppy might've snagged it for Baby Joey before he'd gotten his hands on it.

Annelise walked over to the chair and ran a hand over one of the smooth arms, nudging it into a gentle rocking motion. "It's perfect."

She glanced over at him with a watery smile and then took a deep breath. "I have a boutique for AW GlowCare downtown with an attached laboratory and business office, and I usually spend several hours a day there, so I promise I won't always be in your hair like this."

"You're not an inconvenience, Annelise. I wouldn't have invited you to stay if I didn't want you here." He tipped his head toward the study. "Anything you need or want, you just let me know, okay?"

"I'm not sure how to thank you for all of this. I really don't…" Annelise's voice drifted off, and the light in her eyes warmed him from the inside out all over again.

"No need to thank me." He shook his head and stayed rooted in the doorway. This was her space, and he wanted her to know he respected it.

They weren't a couple, and they never would be, because it was the most sensible decision either of them could make. After all, Annelise was having another man's baby, and Drake prided himself on being a gentleman.

He forced himself to look away from her delicate features and focused on the stuffed panda instead. Its gold plastic eyes seemed to wink at him.

Who did he think he was fooling? Drake could repeat those flimsy excuses all day long in his head, but even he knew better than to believe them.

Chapter Six

The following day, Drake only saw Annelise briefly over coffee before she headed toward the AW GlowCare headquarters for work. They'd spent the evening in their separate rooms, Drake staring up at the ceiling while Annelise watched her favorite television show. Thanks to the surprisingly thin walls in his stately ranch home, Drake now knew exactly who the *Gilmore Girls* were, and he was more than familiar with the la-la-la refrain of the show's theme song.

It was nice having someone else in the house, even if her presence was heard rather than seen. Drake had never liked being in his head too much, and with so much going on in Emerald Ridge, his mind was working overtime trying to figure out who could've gotten their hands on the Gift of Fortune invitations, why someone would've wanted to force a reunion between him and his secret twin, and if either of those things was in any way related to the rash of ranch sabotage in the area in recent months. With Annelise under his roof, his raw nerves were soothed simply by knowing she was there. Safe…secure…happy.

"I guess I'll see you later," she said as she slid her handbag over her shoulder and smoothed her bangs out of her eyes. She was wearing another of those pencil skirts she seemed to favor, and her dark hair was piled on top of her head in a voluminous bun, secured with nothing but an actual pencil, of all things. Paired with her usual stilettos, she was giving off a feminine rocket scientist vibe that Drake found irresistible.

He stared hard into his coffee. "Have a great day. Cameron and I are doing some digging into our adoption today. If we get lucky and catch a lead, I might be home late. Someone on staff from the guest ranch will bring dinner over later, though."

"Drake." She leveled him with a stern look. "I told you that you don't need to spoil me."

"Humor me?" He arched an eyebrow.

She was clearly capable of taking care of herself and her baby while also running her own company, but that didn't mean she had to do everything all on her own. The way Drake saw it, she was overdue for some pampering.

"If you insist." Her lips twitched into a grin. "I'll try and wait for you, though. I don't really like eating alone."

She'd already told him that more often than not, she ate by herself in the big mansion she shared with Courtney. Sometimes living with someone could feel even lonelier than being on your own.

"Fingers crossed you and Cameron find some answers," she said, fluttering her fingertips in a parting wave on her way out.

She somehow seemed to take all the air in the house with her when she left, because Drake's chest constricted the second she was gone, mind reeling with all the possible answers he hoped to uncover with Cameron. Within seconds of her departure, he grabbed his keys and headed out to pick him up.

The Gift of Fortune abode that Cameron was staying at was one of twenty-five guest cabins spread over the property. It had a rustic yet elegant vibe, with a deck that afforded a full three-hundred-sixty-degree view of the ranch, and a fire pit far enough from the trees to avoid trouble in Texas's dry summer climate. When Drake pulled up to the cabin, Cameron was ready and waiting for him, sprawled in one of the Adirondack-style chairs situated under the whirring ceiling fans on the cabin's front porch.

Drake's pulse kicked up a notch as his brother unfolded himself from the chair to walk toward the car. He wondered if he'd ever grow accustomed to the sight of another human being who looked exactly like him. Regular twins had their entire lifetimes together to know each other. Drake and Cameron were running on two days.

He'd read stories about twins developing such a strong connection that they spoke to each other in a secret childhood language or claimed to have some sort of twin telepathy even when they were apart. Somehow, Drake doubted anything like that was in the cards.

"Hey," Cameron said as he settled in the passenger seat and shut the car door.

Drake glanced at his brother's profile, identical to his own. "Hey. How's the guest cabin? Did you sleep okay?"

"Everything was great. This is such a nice place." Cameron shrugged. "As far as sleep, I didn't get much, but that didn't have anything to do with the accommodations. I guess I'm still getting used to everything, you know?"

Oh, Drake knew all right.

"I hear you. I'm not exactly firing on all cylinders today either." He handed his brother a file folder. "Here's the information my parents had tucked away in the safe. I thought we could start at the adoption agency. It's about a forty-five-minute drive from here. I couldn't find them online, so who knows if they're operational anymore. But it's a start…and it's located in a town even smaller than Emerald Ridge. If the rumor mill out there is anything like ours, we might find someone who remembers something."

"'Someone who remembers something.' Well, I suppose desperate times call for desperate measures." Cameron laughed under his breath as he scanned the papers in the slim folder.

All it contained was a contract for a private adoption between Hayden and Darla Fortune and an agency called Texas Royale Private Adoption Agency, along with a copy of Drake's birth certificate. Under Texas state law, once a child was adopted, the original birth certificate was sealed and replaced with a new document containing the names of the adoptive parents in place of the birth parents. The copy of the birth certificate in the file was identical to the one Drake had in his personal records at home. It listed Darla Fortune as his mother, Hayden Fortune as his father and Drake's place of birth as Emerald Ridge. His original birth certificate was no longer accessible in the Texas court system.

The drive passed quickly, with Drake and Cameron exchanging more information about their lives. Cameron seemed amused when Drake told him that the woman who'd labeled him *Drake the Snake* outside the coffee shop was now sharing his house. He passed along Annelise's apology, and Cameron said he hoped things worked out for her, because she'd seemed awfully upset yesterday. Rightfully so, by the sound of things.

Everything was going to work out just fine for Annelise and her baby. Drake would see to it himself.

"You weren't kidding. This looks like the very definition of a one-horse town," Cameron remarked as Drake turned the Porsche off the highway and onto the dusty side road his navigation system indicated would take them straight toward the address listed for Texas Royale Private Adoption Agency on his adoption paperwork. A sad-looking quarter horse gazed at them from a paddock on the corner, ears swiveling at the rumbling sound of the sports car's engine.

Drake's gut churned as they crawled closer to a ramshackle downtown. The place was a virtual ghost town, with as many vacant buildings as there were occupied commercial spaces. In the span of two blocks, they passed a defunct funeral home, a deserted video rental store and a floral shop with the *F* missing from the sign on the awning.

"Maybe someone at the 'lorist' can help us," Cameron said with a snort.

"This place is like a time capsule." Drake gritted his teeth. The idea that they might stumble upon any sort of useful information was starting to feel like a long shot at best.

"We're coming up on the address. It should be right

over here." Cameron pointed to a strip center of several connected businesses.

Nodding, Drake pulled into a parking space directly in front of a dusty glass door that matched the address listed in the file. The place looked like it had been empty for a decade or three.

He peered through the windshield at the vacant office space. "There's no sign. No telling if the adoption agency was even the last business to occupy this space."

"Who knows." Cameron sighed. "There's an open diner a couple doors down. Do you want to try talking to some folks over there?"

"I guess it's worth a shot." They'd come all this way. Drake didn't want to leave any stone unturned, and besides, the diner had a flashing neon sign in the window advertising fresh, warm cinnamon rolls.

The best in the Lone Star State, allegedly.

The sign must've been spot-on, though, because the place was packed, and the air in the diner was thick with the scent of hot sticky buns. Drake's stomach growled as he and his twin snagged the last available booth.

"Welcome." The waitress, a sixtyish-looking woman wearing a sky-blue polyester uniform that resembled a relic from the 1950s, slapped a pair of menus down on the table. She regarded Drake and Cameron over the top of her bifocals. "Well, well. You two are obviously related, and neither of you looks familiar, so you must be visiting."

"We are." Cameron flashed her a grin. "What's good here?"

"The cinnamon rolls. Best in the Lone Star State, just like the sign says. They're as big as your face." She pulled an order pad from the pocket of her apron. "You know what they say. Everything's bigger in Texas."

"We'll take two." Drake handed her his menu. "And I'll have a Texas-sized coffee."

"Same," Cameron echoed.

"Coming right up." She tucked the order pad back into her pocket and the menus under one arm. "My name's Shirley. Anything else I can help you boys with?"

Drake and Cameron exchanged a glance. Now seemed like as good a time as any to start asking questions, especially since she'd basically given them an invitation to do so.

"Actually, the reason we're here is because we were adopted as babies from Texas Royale Private Adoption Agency. Perhaps you're familiar with the place?" Cameron said. "Their office used to be a few doors down from here…"

Shirley's brow furrowed. "Sure, I know the place. I've lived here all my life. I'm afraid you're out of luck, though. That agency closed down years ago. Seems I remember something about them getting in trouble with the state adoption board."

Drake would've been hard-pressed to say he was surprised, given the fact that the agency hadn't informed his parents he had a twin brother who was also available for adoption.

"You don't happen to know anyone else around here who might have more information?" he prompted. "We'd really appreciate it, Shirley."

The waitress gnawed on her pencil eraser for a minute, sizing them up. "Listen, you seem like sweet boys. I'd love to help, but—"

Drake lifted an eyebrow. "But?"

"But I don't want to get anyone in trouble," she said under her breath.

At last, they seemed to be getting somewhere.

Drake held up his hands. "We're not looking for trouble. You have my word. We're just looking for information about our past. That's it."

She shifted from one foot to the other. "Okay, wait here. I have a friend who used to be employed there and might be willing to answer a few questions. Now she works here, back in the kitchen, but she's on the clock. You're going to have to make it quick. The guy who owns this place isn't as sweet as his cinnamon buns, if you get my drift."

Bingo.

Cameron nodded. "We'll only ask a few quick questions. We promise."

Shirley lingered for another second, appearing to mull things over until a booming voice came from the pass-through area between the kitchen and the front of house.

"Order up, Shirley! What's taking so long over there?"

Drake glanced over just in time to see a red-faced man in a white T-shirt slam a spatula down on a silver bell.

"See what I mean." Shirley rolled her eyes. "Sit tight. I'll send her out in a few."

She rapped her knuckles on the table a few times and then left with a curt nod.

"I don't know who scares me more," Cameron quipped after she'd gone. "Shirley or the guy with the spatula."

Drake snorted. "My money's on Shirley."

Before they had time to formulate any sort of plan, another woman stopped at their table and plopped two of the biggest cinnamon rolls Drake had ever seen onto the cracked laminate. Each one was, indeed, the size of his face.

"I'm Alice. Shirley said you have questions about the old adoption agency," she said in a hushed tone. She tucked shaky hands into the pockets of her apron, double-tied around her slender frame.

Like Shirley, Alice looked to be in her mid to late sixties, with cropped silver hair and thin, cracked lips. Deep-set eyes flicked from Drake to Cameron and back again.

Drake sat up a little straighter on his side of the booth. "Alice, thank you for talking to us. My name is Drake Fortune, and this is—"

The older woman cut him off before he could finish. "Wait. Did you say your last name was Fortune?"

"Yes, I—"

She backed away, shaking her head. "Never mind. I told that lady back in May that I don't want anything to do with this, and I meant it. I didn't run that place. I only worked there."

Cameron's eyes flashed. "What lady?"

Drake spoke in as soothing a voice as he could manage. "Alice, please. Clearly, you recognized my name. My brother and I were both adopted from Texas Royale Private Adoption Agency, and we each just found out the other existed a few days ago because someone set us up. We're just trying to find out who is behind all of this and why they're toying in our lives after all these years."

"You're the closest we've come to finding any answers." Cameron's voice was pleading now. "We're not going to get you in any kind of trouble. We promise. Anything you tell us stays between us."

Alice glanced from one brother to the other. "You really just found out you were identical twins a few days ago?"

Drake shook his head.

"That's a shame. Twins should grow up together. I said that all along, even back then. Even when…" Her voice drifted off, and she sighed. "Never mind all that. I'll tell you what you want to know, and then I have to get back to work. But if anyone else turns up, I'll deny I ever said a word."

"Fair," Drake said as he tried to tamp down the dread twisting in his gut. He didn't know what to make of the fact that she'd immediately recognized his name, but it didn't seem good.

Alice took a deep breath. "Like I said, I wasn't in charge of the place. I was the owner's administrative assistant upward of twenty-five years, though, and I kept hard copies of all the files. When legal troubles caused the agency to close, the owner skipped town, so I took the files home. It didn't seem right to just destroy everything. Those boxes have been sitting untouched in the storage shed behind my house for more than a decade. Until two months or so ago…"

"What happened then?" Cameron asked. His leg had started to jiggle under the table, rattling the silverware.

"A lady showed up here looking for me, and she offered me a whole pot of money for the hard copy of Drake Fortune's adoption file." Her eyes flicked toward Drake, regret etched in the lines that were creasing her forehead.

He gasped. "*What?* Who?"

Whoever had bribed Alice into turning over his file had to be the same person responsible for sending Cameron the Gift of Fortune invitation. It was the only thing that made sense.

"She paid in cash and didn't tell me her name. If I had to guess, I'd say she was in her thirties. She had short, dark hair, round glasses, and she wore a big puffy coat." Alice frowned. "That's the part that really stuck out."

"A big puffy coat? In Texas, during early summer?" Cameron blew out a breath. "I can certainly see why that struck you as odd."

Alice nodded. "I gave her the file, and that was that. I never understood why she wanted it in the first place, except for the part about you being a twin. Everything else was standard—the mother was just a young girl who wasn't ready to be a mom, least of all to a set of twins. The Fortunes wanted to adopt because the wife had recently had a miscarriage and was afraid she wouldn't be able to have more children. I swear to you both that's all I know." The woman glanced at the pass-through, where the spatula-wielding man was sliding two more plates onto the metal counter. "I've got to go."

She darted away before Drake or Cameron could say anything else. They sat there, shell-shocked, for a long moment without touching their food.

Her description of the circumstances surrounding Drake's adoption matched everything that Hayden and

Darla had always told him. But no one had known about Cameron. Why would anyone else know, and more importantly, why would they *care*? The only person who might have a vested interest would be their birth mother, but if the stranger who'd bribed Alice was in her thirties, that ruled her out right away.

Finally, Cameron picked up his fork with a sigh. "I don't know anyone who matches the description of the woman who paid Alice to get her hands on your file. Do you?"

Drake shook his head. He'd been racking his brain this entire time, but no one came to mind. Given the puffy coat, he wondered if she could've been trying to disguise her identity.

"Someone came digging for information on you." Cameron pointed at him with his fork. "Whoever it was then found me and lured me to Emerald Ridge."

"I know." Drake's teeth ground together. "But who? And why? And how did she manage to get her hands on a Gift of Fortune invitation?"

They'd managed to track down a lead, but instead of finding answers, they were left with yet more unanswered questions. Why would anyone do any of the strange things that had been going on? And if the culprit could somehow snag a Gift of Fortune invitation from the office at Fortune's Gold Ranch or the main house, did that mean whoever was pulling the puppet strings was someone Drake knew personally?

Maybe even a friend or family member?

The idea seemed unthinkable, but nothing much made sense anymore.

"This is without a doubt the best cinnamon roll

I've ever had," Cameron said, jarring him out of his thoughts. "At least one good thing came from this little day trip…"

Not wanting to be rude, Drake forced a polite smile his brother's way, but this new information was almost too much to take. He picked up his fork, poised to dive in and try to forget everything he'd just heard until he could get home and talk about it with Annelise. Funnily enough, she was the first person he wanted to tell. Not his parents, not his siblings, not his cousins.

Only her.

He didn't want to think about what that meant. Annelise's declaration this morning that she didn't want him spoiling her was the reminder that he'd needed— they were roommates, not soulmates. Those were two very different things.

Drake placed his fork back down on the table without taking a bite. As tempting as the best cinnamon rolls in the Lone Star State sounded, he just didn't have much of an appetite anymore.

Chapter Seven

Annelise spent most of the day tucked away in the lab at AW GlowCare, losing herself in her work. Still, thoughts of Drake kept sneaking their way into her consciousness. Before she left for the day, she made him a gift basket filled with all their best men's products. The poor guy needed a little pampering. He'd been trying to fix everyone's problems lately, including hers. For once, she wanted to take care of him instead of the other way around.

That was a perfectly normal thought for a friend to have about another friend, wasn't it?

Perhaps...except you spent a large part of yesterday thinking about kissing *said friend.*

Annelise wasn't sure how it happened. One minute, they'd been eating cake. The next, her appetite had... shifted. Significantly. She'd wanted to devour the man as if he'd been slathered in buttercream frosting.

This was all Drake's fault. He was being far too nice to her. No one had showered her with such tender loving care since her father passed away. Brad certainly hadn't. She'd forgotten what it felt like to have someone on her side…to not feel all alone in the world. It was a heady experience, and it made her want to rethink her vow to never trust a man again as long as she lived.

Which was precisely why she needed the vow to begin with.

Annelise propped the gift basket on the kitchen counter where the cake had sat the day before. Then she arranged two place settings on the bar with place-mats and dishes she found while exploring the kitchen. The bar seemed like a much more casual, innocent lo-cation to have dinner together than, say, the formal din-ing room with its dramatic mood lighting and sparkling crystal chandelier.

Drake had seriously undersold the magnificence of his home. True, the square footage wasn't anywhere near that of the mansion she shared with Courtney at Wellington Ranch. But Annelise considered that a good thing. Her spacious family home had been lovely back when it was exactly that: a *family* home. She and Jax had shared an idyllic childhood there, even though he'd al-ways insisted she was naive and only saw the good parts about their upbringing. That was the thing, though—she truly didn't carry any bad memories from that time. *All* of it had been made up of good parts.

Then her mother had passed away, and shortly after-ward, her father had met Courtney. Now Daddy was gone too, and the house felt more like a mausoleum than a home.

Drake's house was the perfect size—roomy enough for everyone to have their own space, yet at the same time cozy enough to know she wasn't there all by her-self. Just the sound of Drake padding around in his sock feet made her sleep better at night. It was crazy, she knew.

So, so crazy, she whispered to herself as she adjusted the bow on his gift basket. Just as Drake said, someone from Fortune's Gold Ranch and Spa had delivered dinner and left reheating instructions for her while she'd been at work. Not just dinner, but a three-course gourmet meal, complete with appetizers and desserts. If Annelise didn't know better, she might've thought Drake had let the kitchen know she was eating for two.

He wouldn't do that, though. He'd been nothing but discreet about her little secret. Still, she was going to need some serious help eating all this food.

Fortunately, Drake walked through the front door just as she was pulling the main course from the oven.

"Wow." He came to a stop near the kitchen counter and glanced around. "What's all this?"

"Dinner." Annelise went to work plating the food. "You sound surprised. Aren't you the one who arranged all this?"

"I made arrangements for the food." He waved a hand, encompassing the place settings and the gift basket. "Not all of this. I have to admit, it's a nice surprise to come home to."

"Good." Nerves fluttered through Annelise as she removed the pot holders from her hands. She had no reason at all to feel anxious. It was just Drake…her *friend*. "I hope you're hungry. I'm starved, and I can't wait to hear about your day. You and Cameron were gone for quite a while. Did you learn anything useful?"

Drake removed his Stetson and set it on a side table as he dragged a hand through his blond hair. It wasn't until he came closer that she noticed the lines around his eyes seemed deeper.

"Drake?" Her stomach tumbled. "What's wrong? Did something else bad happen? You didn't lose any more horses or cattle, did you?"

He rested his hands on her shoulders and gave them a reassuring squeeze. "Don't worry. It's nothing like that. Let's just say that today was an eye-opener."

She regarded him with a huff. "Stop that."

He dropped his hands back to his sides. "Stop what?"

"Stop downplaying whatever is going on. I can tell you're stressed, and you're trying to protect me from whatever it is. Just because I'm pregnant doesn't mean I'm a delicate little daisy."

His lips quirked into a half grin. "Annelise, trust me. I know better than to think that. You're one of the strongest, most capable people I know. Also, Cameron is still a bit afraid of you, so a delicate little daisy is probably the last flower I would compare you with."

She tipped her chin up to meet his gaze. She'd kicked off her stilettos when she'd gotten home, and in his boots, he was a good six inches taller than she was. "Which flower would you choose, then?"

It was a silly question, only intended to call him out because he did treat her like a delicate little daisy sometimes. Ordinarily, she didn't really mind. But she could tell whatever had happened today had gotten under his skin, and she wanted to help. Friendship was supposed to work both ways.

"Let's see." He studied her just enough for her cheeks to go warm. "If you were a flower, I believe you'd be a daylily."

"A daylily?" Annelise knew very little about daylilies. Or gardening in general. For all she knew, daylilies were even more fragile than daisies. "Why?"

"Because they're beautiful and resilient, and they manage to bloom no matter what nature throws their way," he said, arching a brow.

Oh. She gulped.

"That sounds lovely, but…" She needed to say something to diffuse the situation. He'd only just gotten home, and already she was thinking about kissing him again. "Don't daylilies only bloom for a day? I thought that's how they got their name."

"That just makes them all the more precious. Blink and you'll miss them." He slid his big hands down her arms until his fingers wove through hers. Then he tugged her closer until she could see the tiny gold flecks in his blue eyes, shimmering like hidden treasure. Fortune's gold. "I pity any man who looks away and misses such a spectacular show."

He meant Brad, obviously, but Annelise was suddenly having trouble remembering her ex's name. Or that he'd ever existed.

"Good answer?" Drake asked, tenderness replacing the weariness she'd seen in his expression only moments before.

"*Great* answer," she whispered.

He pressed a gentle kiss to the top of her head— an innocent gesture that shouldn't have seemed so intimate…so utterly charming. Somehow it did, and it made Annelise *feel* like a flower. Blossoming from the inside out.

"I'm glad." He winked. "Now, let's sit down for a nice dinner, and I'll tell you everything."

Drake told Annelise all about his fact-finding mission with Cameron while they ate, and he didn't spare any details. She wanted to hear everything, so he laid it all out, from the florist sign with the missing *F* to Angry Spatula Guy to the startling news that someone had recently paid Alice "a whole pot of money" for the hard copy of his adoption files.

They'd just polished off dessert when he'd gotten to that part. Annelise's eyes were huge in her face as she placed her napkin down beside her empty plate.

"Drake, this entire story is *crazy*." She shook her head.

"Believe me, I know." His mind was still reeling from everything they'd discovered. All the drama that had taken place around Emerald Ridge lately had to mean something. But what? "Before we left the diner, I poked around online and found out some really troubling information on Texas Royale Private Adoption Agency. The waitress we talked to mentioned they'd been in trouble with the state adoption board, and when I searched their database, I was able to find a few articles that hadn't popped up in the general search I did before our trip."

Annelise gasped. "Oh, no. What did you discover?"

"Apparently, they charged an absolute fortune in adoption fees, much higher than the standard rate. The agency was suspended for predatory policies aimed at taking advantage of wealthy couples who were desperate for children." Drake paused to take a tense inhale. That certainly explained why he and Cameron had both been placed with such affluent families. Still, he couldn't help but wonder how different his life might have been if they'd been adopted together instead of separately. "The agency's most glaring violation of state law was their policy of always splitting up twins in order to get the most money possible from two separate families. The hopeful parents never had any idea they were adopting a baby who had a twin. It's what eventually got the agency shut down. The state of Texas always aims to place twins together when possible."

"Drake, that's awful. I'm so sorry." Annelise placed her hand on top of his. "There's got to be a way to get to the bottom of this. Alice said the woman who came to see her about the files looked like she was in her thirties?"

He nodded. "With short, dark hair, round glasses and a puffy coat."

"Like a down, ski-type coat? Honestly, that might be the weirdest part. Who wears a puffer coat in Texas this time of year?"

"Agreed." Drake rubbed his temples. "I can't stop thinking about it. I don't know a single person who matches that description."

"I can't think of anyone who looks like that either." Annelise sighed. "I'm sorry, Drake. I wish I could do more to help."

"What are you talking about? You're helping just by being here. By listening…" He meant every word. In fact, he'd spent the entire drive home looking forward to seeing her. He hadn't even taken the time to update his family, because the only person he felt like talking to was waiting for him at home.

This was getting dangerous. She'd only been here for a day and a half, and already he was dreading the day she decided to leave.

"That doesn't really feel like helping," she countered, and something about the way she was looking at him was like a truth serum.

His blood felt like sweet honey flowing through his veins. Surely it wouldn't hurt to tell her how he really felt. Honesty was good. It's what friends did...they told each other the raw, unfiltered truth.

"Trust me, it helps. There's no one else I'd rather talk to about any of this. No one else I'd rather see at the end of a day like today," Drake said quietly.

No one I'd rather touch...no one I'd rather kiss...

Annelise's eyes went liquid, and he wondered for a second if she could read his mind. Or maybe not, and she was simply thinking the same thing. *Wanting* the same thing.

He wasn't going to make the first move, though. If anything happened between them, he wanted her to be sure. He tried to tell himself it was because he couldn't possibly have real feelings for her. She was a sweet person. It was only natural for him to feel so protective of her after his friend had let her down so badly.

But the part of him that wasn't in complete denial told him the reason he didn't want to be the first one to step a toe over the line was because she was starting to mean something to him. Possibly a little too much.

He shouldn't be having these kinds of thoughts about his friend's pregnant ex. Drake wasn't even sure who he was anymore. His entire identity had been thrown into a tailspin, and now he was teetering on the edge of falling too hard. *Much* too fast.

Was he the type of guy to catch feelings for a woman who, up until recently, belonged to his friend? What would happen if Brad came to his senses and popped up in Emerald Ridge, ready for a fresh start with Annelise? Would she take him back?

Warning bells were going off in every corner of Drake's mind, but he was flagrantly ignoring each and every one of them. His pulse was pounding so hard he could feel it in his throat. No woman had ever had this kind of effect on him before. It was as unsettling as it was provocative.

"Drake," she whispered, and his name sounded like a prayer falling from her lips. Or a question…or possibly both.

The answer was a given.

"Yes," he said, and before he'd even finished forming the word, she'd climbed off her barstool, wrapped her slender arms around his neck and pressed her lips to his.

Her mouth was warm and sweet—sweeter than he could've possibly imagined, even after admittedly spending a night…*or two*…picturing this moment in his head. That had just been pure fantasy, though, and the Annelise in his arms was very much real.

"You're still doing it," she whispered against his mouth, and the warmth of her breath set every nerve ending in his body on fire.

"What am I doing?" he asked without opening his eyes.

What *was* he doing? What were *they* doing? This wasn't supposed to be happening.

"You're still treating me like a delicate little daisy," Annelise murmured. "I'm a daylily, remember?"

It was all the permission he needed to deepen the kiss, and in an instant it switched from being a tentative exploration to something more…potent. Something as lush and unstoppable as those fleeting blooms reaching for the sky with wild abandon.

It was without a doubt the hottest kiss Drake Fortune had ever known.

The intensity of it caught them both off guard, and at the same moment, they both pulled away to stare at each other as if they'd just been struck by lightning.

"W-what was that?" Annelise asked in a shaky breath. "I mean, I know it was a kiss, but—"

But it was more than just a kiss. It was everything. And now Drake knew without a doubt that they'd both felt it, all the way down to their toes.

He ran the pad of his thumb over her bottom lip. Gently…reverently. It was swollen, and he wanted nothing more than to capture her mouth with his again. But there was no doubt whatsoever where that would lead.

Drake wrapped a gentle hand around the back of her neck and pulled her close to press his lips against her temple. And they stayed that way for a long moment, catching their respective breaths and trying to make sense of what had just happened.

But maybe there was *no* explaining it. After all, romantic chemistry wasn't an exact science, like what Annelise did in the lab. It was wild and unpredictable… and damned if it didn't make her even more irresistible.

She extricated herself from his arms and squared her

shoulders. "That was...*wow*. But maybe for right now, we should do something else."

That sounded like a completely awful idea to Drake, but he nodded. He'd rather run five hundred miles in the punishing Texas heat with his boots on than do anything to make her feel uncomfortable.

"What did you have in mind?" He folded his arms across his chest to ensure he kept his hands to himself.

"I brought you a little something home from work." She slid the huge gift basket that he'd spied propped at the end of the kitchen bar closer toward him. "It's a selection of AW GlowCare products. I thought you might need a little self-care."

If things around Emerald Ridge and Fortune's Gold Ranch got any crazier, Drake was going to need *a lot* of self-care. As it was, he didn't even know where to start.

He plucked a container of some sort of cream from the basket and turned it over in his hands, impressed by the elegant packaging. "It amazes me that this is what you do for a living. How did you get started?"

"Believe it or not, I was originally inspired by the hot springs right here in Emerald Ridge." She nodded at the product he was holding. "That's one of our bestsellers. Would you like me to show you how to use it?"

"Sure." He handed her the fancy pot of lotion.

She took it, unscrewed the lid and then placed it on the bar. Then her gaze met his again. "Close your eyes."

Drake obeyed, even though he wasn't sure why shutting his eyes was necessary for lotion application. Then again, he was a man—a man who lived on a ranch in Texas—and therefore, his skin care routine consisted of little more than soap and water. What did he know?

"Try and relax," she said as she began massaging his temples.

At first, Drake wasn't sure he could—not with Annelise so perilously close. But after a minute or two, he grew accustomed to the feel of her gentle caress, and he sank into the calming rhythm of her hands moving across his face.

"Whatever that is, it smells fantastic," he murmured.

"That's the lavender and chamomile essential oils. They help relieve stress, anxiety and restlessness," Annelise whispered, and her warm breath fanned across his cheek. "Does it feel like they're working at all?"

Oddly enough, they did. "This is actually very soothing."

"You don't have to sound so surprised," she said, but he could hear the smile in her voice.

"You know what I mean. You've built a massively successful business, all on your own. You clearly know what you're doing. I just never take the time for this sort of thing," he admitted.

"Maybe you should." Annelise's fingertips moved in languid circles over his forehead. "I bet you haven't realized what you're missing."

"You're right. I haven't." Drake's eyes drifted open. "But I think I get it now."

Her gaze fixed on his, and her lips parted slightly. They weren't talking about skin care anymore, and they both knew it.

"This product is made with water from the Emerald Ridge hot spring. You've heard the legend about the spring and its waters, right?" Her hands shifted to the sides of his face, moving in a light, sweeping, upward motion.

Drake groaned under his breath. How did this feel so good? "It's supposed to have healing powers, isn't it."

"Legend says it's also supposed to help with decision-making," she said quietly, running her hands over his eyelids to force his eyes closed again. Her touch was as gentle as the flutter of butterfly wings.

He was seconds away from falling asleep sitting straight up, lulled into relaxation. Drake had a lot of decisions to make—what to do about the ranch sabotage, where to search for clues in the increasingly mysterious appearance of Baby Joey, how to find the puzzling woman in the puffer coat who'd been digging into his past.

Maybe the legend about the hot spring was right. Everything somehow felt more manageable now, save for the most pressing decision of all...

What to do about his growing feelings for Annelise.

Chapter Eight

Annelise tiptoed around Drake for the rest of the week, lest she lose her head and kiss him again.

What a mistake that had been.

It had seemed so natural at first, as easy and instinctual as breathing. Being around Drake always felt that way. He was just so nice and thoughtful that he made her feel instantly at ease all the time. *Too* at ease, apparently, since she'd only been living in his house for two days before she nearly climbed him like one of the towering oak trees that lined the scenic driveway of Fortune's Gold Ranch.

The kiss had started out innocently enough—tender and sweet. Then she'd asked him for more, and boy, had he delivered. She hadn't been ready...then again, in what world would it have been possible to be ready for a kiss like that? Clearly every man she'd ever been with had been holding out on her. Annelise hadn't realized that a simple lip-lock could be so powerful...so completely and utterly disarming. Drake had made her feel things she hadn't known she was capable of feeling. Her heart had nearly burst right out of her chest, and the ache that had instantly hit her low in her belly *still* hadn't completely gone away. Every time she looked at him, it came roaring back in full force.

On Monday, she'd come home from work to find a pregnancy book waiting for her on top of her bed. It was the very one she'd mentioned in passing the day before, about what to expect for each month of pregnancy. Then two days later, he'd surprised her with one of those ergonomic pregnancy body pillows everyone raved about. Both gifts had been tied with mint-green satin ribbons, the exact color she'd been contemplating for a nursery, assuming she figured out where she was going to be living when she gave birth.

It still seemed so far away. She had another six months of pregnancy to navigate.

But then yesterday, Drake had stunned her with another gift. This one was a bassinet that matched the antique rocker in her bedroom. She tried to tell him she really had no business using Fortune family heirlooms, but he'd insisted. He wanted her to feel like she was still part of a family, even though both her parents had passed on, and that simple statement had been enough to melt her heart in ten different ways.

Drake understood her. He paid attention to every little thing she said, because he cared. Brad had never once treated her with such thoughtfulness, and Annelise had been ready to *marry* him. Giving in to temptation and opening herself up to Drake should've been a no-brainer.

Pregnancy magnified everything. That was the problem. A kiss wasn't just a kiss anymore. Not now that she was going to be a mother.

Her brother, Jax, was right. She was too naive…too trusting. She couldn't make those same mistakes anymore, because now she wasn't the only one who'd suffer the consequences if she put her faith in the wrong person. It wasn't just her life that she had to think about anymore, but also her child's.

Nothing in the entire world was more important than her baby.

But day after day, Drake kept showing himself to be a stand-up guy. And heaven help her, even all those years of wearing sky-high stilettos hadn't prepared her for quite this much tiptoeing. She was one crinkly-eyed smile and tip of his Stetson away from kicking off her heels once and for all.

It was a relief on Friday afternoon when she got home after work and Drake's Porsche wasn't parked in the circular drive. *Finally.* There was so much pent-up longing in his house that the atmosphere was more charged than the Emerald Ridge hot spring. She just needed a minute—or ten—to catch her breath.

Annelise let herself in the front door and glanced around, just in case. "Drake?"

He was usually home this time of day. She suspected he'd rearranged his schedule so she wouldn't have to spent much time alone, which she actually loved since living with Courtney had made her feel so lonely at times. She just loved it a little too much, that's all.

But today, when Annelise called out to him, there was no answer. No broad-shouldered cowboy greeting her with a treat from Emerald Ridge Bakery. No crooked smile as he threatened to buy another giant panda because of their running joke that the first one needed a friend. No prolonged eye contact that made her go all swoony when she least expected it.

She should've been relieved. This was what she'd been hoping for all week long. At least, she'd thought it was. She wasn't sure why the sinking sensation in the pit of her stomach felt so much like disappointment.

You're being ridiculous. You're a grown woman, and you can spend an evening by yourself. You did it every single day when you lived with Courtney.

Guilt pricked Annelise's consciousness. She hadn't called or checked in on her stepmother since the day she'd moved out. Granted, the telephone worked both ways, and Courtney hadn't reached out to her either. But what would her father think? Just because she wasn't particularly fond of the woman didn't mean she should completely ignore her indefinitely.

She'd call her first thing tomorrow morning, as painfully awkward as it might be. Tonight, she was going to have a nice soak with her favorite AW GlowCare bubble bath infused with elderflower and ripe strawberry and manage to entertain herself without thinking about Drake Fortune or his current whereabouts.

Easy-peasy.

But as Annelise neared her suite, she noticed a faint chemical smell coming from her bedroom. Her nose twitched as she grew closer. The door to her bedroom was propped open, and she could see the gossamer curtains billowing in the breeze, as if someone had opened the windows.

Her footsteps slowed. Then her mouth went dry as she thought about the vandals who'd been attacking ranches in and around Emerald Ridge. What if they'd broken into her suite?

Surely that couldn't be true. Thus far, the saboteurs had mostly been cutting fences and breaking into barns. With the exception of the heirloom statue that had been stolen from Jonathan Porter's mansion last month, they'd been targeting ranch operations, not personal residences.

Even so, she reached into her handbag for her cell phone and dialed Drake's number, just in case. She was a grown-up who was going to have to learn to fully take care of herself if she planned on raising a child all alone, but she didn't want to walk into a trap unprepared. If she was about to surprise the criminals, someone needed to know her whereabouts.

The line started to ring just as she stepped inside the bedroom. Relief coursed through her when she realized she was still alone, but then her heart beat hard against her ribs when she spotted the adjoining study. Her hand, still clutching the cell phone, fell away from her ear as she walked slowly into the suite's smaller room.

Someone—Drake, obviously—had transformed the cozy space while she'd been in her lab all afternoon. The walls, previously a neutral eggshell hue, were now tinted a serene mint green. It was just the right color, even prettier in person than it had been on the digital paint chips she'd been perusing online.

A lump formed in Annelise's throat as her free hand moved to her belly. Drake had gone out, bought the supplies and painted the walls to surprise her. She could tell he'd done it himself, because his platinum Rolex was sitting on the changing table, another new addition, along with an extra unused paintbrush. A crib stood along the far wall, next to a small pile of drop cloths and painting supplies. The furniture seemed new, and it was a beautiful Chantilly cream color that matched the room's trim, the perfect complement to the soothing mint walls.

Annelise turned a slow circle, taking it all in. Her baby had a nursery—a *home*. And it looked exactly the way she'd pictured it in her head, only now it was real.

Everything was real. She was having a baby. Of course she'd known that all along, but now, standing in the pretty little room, reality truly sank in. She was going to be a mother. And just like Lorelai and Rory Gilmore, she and her baby were going to be on their own, but for the first time, Annelise knew in her heart it was all going to be okay. *They* were going to be okay, because even though Brad was out of the picture, they weren't truly alone. They had Drake, and they had this lovely room on this lovely ranch...

Then the same old doubts hit her like a punch to the gut. She couldn't possibly trust this extravagant gesture. Offering to let her stay with him was one thing, but decorating a nursery and inviting her to raise her baby here was another thing entirely. Why would Drake want that? This entire arrangement was only supposed to be temporary.

Wasn't it?

You feel at home now, her thoughts screamed. *But just wait. He'll leave you high and dry in the end, just like Brad. What man would possibly want to play house in this scenario?*

A tear slipped down her cheek. Then another...and another.

"Hello? *Hello?*"

Annelise sniffed and glanced at the forgotten phone in her hand. She'd been so distracted by the painted nursery that the call had completely slipped her mind. Pregnancy brain for the win.

"Hello? Drake?" she said into the phone.

But when he repeated his greeting, his voice seemed to be coming at her in stereo. "Hello, mama-to-be."

Annelise whipped her head around, and there he was, standing right behind her with his phone pressed to his ear.

"You weren't supposed to beat me home." He arched a single eyebrow, and a tender smile tipped his lips. "Surprise."

Annelise let her phone slip from her fingers as she ran straight toward him and threw her arms around his neck. The tears came hot and fast as she cried against the soft chambray fabric of his Western-style shirt.

"Hey there, now. Don't cry, sweetheart. Please." He shoved his phone into his jeans pocket and ran his hands in soothing circles over her back. "Whatever it is, we can fix it. I promise. Did I get the color wrong?"

She shook her head.

"The color is *perfect*," she whispered against his strong and steady shoulder. She didn't want to let him go. As foolish as it was, she wanted to let herself believe in this crazy fantasy—if only for the moment. "I love it. It's exactly what I wanted."

"Well, thank heaven for that." His laugh rumbled through Annelise. "You scared me, sweetheart."

She wanted to tell him to never stop calling her that, but she couldn't form any words. Since the start of her pregnancy, she'd been trying so hard to keep her emotions at bay. Annelise had only cracked twice—first, when she'd thrown her cranberry juice in Brad's face at Captain's restaurant on her birthday after he'd dumped her, and then again when she'd yelled at Cameron Waite on the street and called him Drake the Snake.

Now she was breaking in a different way—one that was far more frightening, because it was her vulnerable heart that was on full display this time instead of her anger.

Drake unwound her arms from his neck and held both her hands tightly as he pressed his forehead to hers and searched her gaze. "Talk to me, Annelise. What's going on in that gorgeous head of yours?"

Dare she say what she was really thinking? He'd just painted a room in his house and given her a nursery. It was the most permanent commitment any man in her life had ever made, including her baby's father.

"You really and truly want us to stay, don't you?" she whispered.

Why, though? Had he lost his mind? When would this wonderful man come to his senses?

A quiet smile tugged at his lips until it seemed to take up his entire handsome face. "I do."

Heaven help her, she believed him. And even though a part of her wanted to tell him there was no way she could take advantage of his kindness and stay with him for the entire duration of her pregnancy, a bigger part of her wanted to think that a happy-ever-after was possible. So she pretended they just might have a future together as she smiled and took him at his word.

"What have I done to deserve all this?" she whispered against his lips, heart beating furiously. "What have I done to deserve *you*, Drake Fortune?"

"You deserve the world, darlin'." He pressed a tender kiss to the corner of her lips and hope stirred deep inside her. Foolish, foolish hope. "Will you let me give it to you?"

"Yes," she started to say, but the word was swallowed up in a kiss that made her knees buckle.

He was so warm and strong and solid...how could she resist? The idea that he might leave someday seemed impossible when he touched her like this. So she held on tight and opened up for him, bit by bit, breath by breath...

She'd never wanted a man so badly in her life.

"Drake," she murmured, and her fingertips moved to his belt buckle.

"Yes, baby?" he said, and the words rumbled through her like a tiny earthquake. And for once, it felt good to lose her balance and let herself fall.

"Take me to bed," she said before she could stop herself. She didn't *want* to stop. Not this time. "Please."

She was so ready that she didn't even give him time to answer. Her lips found his, and as she kissed him, her naivete fell away like an unbuttoned dress pooling at her feet. She knew full well what to expect this time, and she wanted it. She wanted *him*—every last part of him that he was willing to give her.

"Are you sure about this?" he murmured as he buried his hands in her hair, eyes blazing into hers.

"I've never been more sure," she breathed.

Then Drake Fortune swept her off her feet, carried her to his bed and gave her his all.

* * *

Drake had never been a big believer in legends. He couldn't even remember a time during his childhood when he'd truly thought Santa Claus was real. Time and again, he'd marveled at his siblings' ability to suspend disbelief.

Flying reindeer, seriously?

Couldn't his brother and sister recognize Darla Fortune's handwriting on the gift tags that were supposedly written by Santa? If the Easter Bunny was real, why did the boxed chocolate rabbits in their matching Easter baskets look so much like the ones he'd seen for sale at Emerald Ridge Grocery downtown? Was it supposed to be a coincidence that the five-dollar bill the tooth fairy left under his pillow in first grade had the same tear in the upper right-hand corner as the one he'd seen in his dad's money clip earlier that morning?

Maybe it was growing up knowing he'd been adopted, but Drake knew better than to put his faith in fairy tales. He'd always had his feet firmly planted in the real world.

Somehow, though, over the course of the past week, he'd almost begun to believe that the legend of the Emerald Ridge hot spring was rooted in fact. As crazy as it was, Annelise's fancy potion had brought Drake clarity. He'd made up his mind…

He wanted Annelise.

Logic told him the feeling was only fleeting. She was a beautiful woman. Of course he wanted to be with her. But that hot spring legend had him believing that he didn't just want her for a night. He wanted more…much more. He'd tried telling himself that legends weren't verifiable. Believing that a lotion could have this much power over him was bonkers.

But then he'd gone to the hardware store to pick up the mint-green paint this morning, and the old man working the paint counter had been some sort of guru when it came to paint colors and their meanings. While the gallon of semigloss had been shaking in the mixing machine, he'd casually told Drake that mint green symbolized serenity and new beginnings.

Nothing could've been more perfect for Annelise and her baby. If Drake had been capable of giving her those two things on a silver platter, he would've done so in a heartbeat. Alas, the best he could do was a minty-green nursery.

He hadn't expected the surprise to move her the way it did. He definitely hadn't expected her to ask him to take her to bed. But of course he wanted her. He wanted her more with each passing day—so much that he could barely think straight. She'd been giving him a wide berth since the night they kissed. Then she'd cried in his arms in the mint-green room, and at long last, the dam between them had broken.

He'd thought it had finally crumbled for good. Long after they'd made love and fallen asleep, tangled in bedsheets, the memory of her honeyed voice played in the back of his head like a dream.

I've never been more sure.

Drake reached for her in the darkness, missing the weight of her head on his shoulder, but the space beside him was empty. The sheets, cold to the touch. He sat up and opened his eyes, but Annelise was nowhere to be seen.

Dread pooled in the pit of his stomach as he climbed out of bed and slid into a pair of pajama bottoms. He told himself she'd probably just gone to the kitchen for a drink of water, but it felt like a lie. And when he left the bedroom, the first place he went looking for her was her suite.

And there he found her, tucked into her bed all alone.

She looked so beautiful bathed in moonlight from the opened windows. Her thick hair was fanned out over her pillow like a dark halo, but the tiny furrow in her brow as she slept told him all he needed to know.

She was afraid. He knew without a doubt that she'd meant it when she'd told him she was sure. He'd been there. She'd opened up to him like a flower, and in that moment, it had been just the two of them. No one else— no painful losses, no broken hearts. But while he'd been sleeping, the real world had crept into his bed and sent her running scared.

"What's it going to take to get you to trust me, sweetheart?" he whispered.

Annelise didn't stir, and it was just as well. She needed her rest. Drake didn't want her to think he was angry or upset that she'd fled back to her room. He wasn't. More than anything, he was sad.

Sad, and just a little bit afraid himself. He didn't want her to retreat and tell him they should go back to being platonic friends. The truth was, Drake didn't know if he could.

Not anymore.

Chapter Nine

Annelise woke with a start, confused at first about where she was.

She'd reached for Drake before she opened her eyes, longing for the feel of his strong arms around her again, but there was no one beside her. It took a moment or two to remember that she'd snuck out of his bed and returned to her room. When she opened her eyes, the first thing her gaze landed on was the pretty mint-green nursery wall, and she felt like crying all over again.

She was a mess.

Poor Drake. He'd been nothing but wonderful to her, and now he probably thought she'd changed her mind again and just wanted to be friends.

Annelise hadn't changed her mind, though. She'd been sure last night, just like she'd said. She was *still* sure…sure that she might be falling for Drake Fortune. And that undeniable truth terrified her to the bone.

The simple act of admitting it to herself made her mouth go as dry as sandpaper. She'd thought she loved Brad, and look how that had turned out.

The comparison was hardly fair. Drake and Brad

were two very different men, and Annelise knew now that she'd never really loved her ex. Even in their best of times, her feelings for him paled in comparison to the way she felt about Drake. Sometimes she wondered if she'd convinced herself she loved Brad because the idea of truly falling in love was simply too frightening to contemplate. Losing her parents had knocked the wind right out of her. She wasn't sure she could live through that sort of loss again. It was better to be safe and settle for less. That way, she'd never truly get hurt.

Brad had hurt her, but he hadn't broken her. Not completely...not the way she'd shatter if she ever let herself love Drake, only to lose him in the end.

Annelise pulled the sheets around her as her breath caught in her throat. She couldn't think about losing Drake. It filled her with panic. It was better to have him in her life as a friend than not have him in it at all. Even if it wasn't what she wanted. She wanted *all* of him, but how would that even work?

Neither of them had really thought it through. No one in Emerald Ridge even knew she was pregnant yet. What were people going to say when they found out that she and Drake were a couple and she was carrying another man's baby? What were the Fortunes going to say? Hadn't they been through enough turmoil already in recent months?

She dropped her head in her hands. Annelise knew exactly what his family would think—they'd tell Drake to run for the hills. They'd say she was vulnerable and desperate for companionship and that she was taking advantage of him and his kindness. She knew this because in her worst moments, she feared those things were true.

You're falling for him, and you know it. Stop pushing him away and trust your feelings for once.

Oh, but that was so much easier said than done. No matter how she felt, Drake deserved better than Annelise and her immense amount of baggage. It was only a matter of time until he woke up and realized that.

"I'm sorry."

They were the first words she said to him after she'd gotten dressed and found Drake in the kitchen, pouring a tall glass of freshly squeezed orange juice.

He kissed her on the cheek as he handed her the juice. "I'm not."

He was being far too nice. This would be so much easier if he would confront her about sending so many mixed messages. She certainly deserved it.

"I didn't mean I was sorry about last night...about what happened between us." She shook her head and stared down into the pulpy liquid in the glass. There was no way she was going to get through what she needed to say if she looked him in the eyes. "I meant I was sorry about going back to my room in the middle of the night, and I'm sorry about—"

"Don't say it." Drake shook his head as he leaned his backside against the kitchen counter, gripping the edges of the hard granite until his knuckles turned white. "Please don't say it, Annelise."

She had to, though. The longer she put it off, the harder it would be. "I'm sorry, but I think I should go back to the Wellington Ranch for a day or two."

Once she'd gotten the words out, she lifted her gaze to his, and the pain in his eyes was an arrow straight to her heart.

"You don't need to do that. This is your home for as long as you want it. I'll give you all the space you need. I promise." Drake's voice broke on that last word, and something inside Annelise broke right along with it.

What was she doing? He was the best thing that had ever happened to her, and she was letting her fears and insecurities get the better of her. She didn't want to go back and live with Courtney, and she really didn't want her child to grow up in that lonely environment. The mansion wasn't a home anymore. Annelise had been staying there in a desperate attempt to hold on to the memories of her parents, but it no longer reminded her of Mom and Dad. It just felt…empty.

She wanted her baby to take its first steps right here, at Fortune's Gold Ranch, in the soothing mint-green room that she loved so much.

"It's not permanent," Annelise assured him. "I think I just need to go back to see how it feels there."

And to see if I am really and truly in love with you.

Drake's eyes bore into hers, like he knew exactly what she was thinking. "I don't want you to go. I—"

She held up a hand. If he said he was falling in love with her too, she'd never get over it. Never, ever. "My trust is low right now, Drake. Before I can really be with someone, I need to figure this out."

"You can figure it out here." His gaze darted toward the floor-to-ceiling windows in the living room. Beyond the glass, cows munched on emerald-green grass in the soft morning light, and a slow-moving image flashed in Annelise's mind like a scene from a movie—her child learning to ride a pony right here in this sacred place, with Drake holding on to the reins.

That was just a fantasy, though. It would never be real. *Why not?*

The question burned into her, daring her to stay put.

"Or better yet, *we* can figure it out. *Together.* Let me be here for you, Annelise. You don't have to do everything all on your own." Drake took a step toward her, and she knew if she let him touch her again, she'd never walk out the door.

And then what would happen? Would she wake up in the middle of the night and freak out again? Would the rest of the Fortunes stage an intervention to try and get Drake to come to his senses?

"I need to get going. Regardless of whether I stay here tonight or not, I need to go to Wellington Ranch this morning to check on things. I feel bad that I haven't communicated with Courtney at all since I've been here." Annelise finished her juice and set the empty glass down on the counter. "I'll think about things, I promise."

"Please be careful. I'm here, and I'm not going anywhere," Drake said, and the glimmer of hope in his smile was bittersweet. "I'll see you later."

Annelise somehow made it to Wellington Ranch without having to pull the car over for a cry. She loved being at Drake's, but she needed to keep her head clear so she could be a good mother and not fall head over heels again and end up brokenhearted. She just needed to get away for a bit. Surely once she was away from Fortune's Gold Ranch, she'd be able to find some clarity.

A heaviness settled over her as she steered her car into the sweeping driveway of the Wellington mansion.

When the house came into view, it was almost like seeing it for the first time. She'd only been gone for a week, and already she felt like a stranger here.

She switched off the ignition and took a deep breath. *Just go inside and see how it feels. Maybe it won't be so bad.* She'd grown up here, after all. Annelise and Jax had both loved the ranch as kids.

Annelise nearly knocked at the front door, and then decided that was ridiculous. Even though she'd moved out, she was still a Wellington. And her family home was still technically her permanent address. So she let herself in, and the huge front door opened with a creak.

A shiver went up and down her spine. She didn't know why she was being so dramatic.

"Courtney?" she called out. "It's me, Annelise. Are you here?"

The only response was her own voice echoing off the foyer's marble floors. That didn't mean much, though. Courtney's wing was pretty far away. If the door to her suite was closed, she probably wouldn't have heard a thing.

Annelise lifted her handbag onto her shoulder and grabbed onto the railing of the curved staircase. She might as well go check and see if Courtney was up there before she went to her own wing to…do what exactly? Decide if she could stand living here for the rest of her life?

One step at a time, she told herself as she climbed the stairs. She didn't have to figure everything out all at once. The important thing was putting some much-needed distance between her and Drake.

Mission accomplished. She hated it already, but she'd done it.

"Courtney?" she called again once she'd reached the second floor and headed down the long hallway that led to the wing containing her stepmother's suite, which consisted of a sitting room, a bedroom, and a spacious master bathroom with an attached closet and dressing room.

Annelise's wing was on the opposite end of the house, designed in an exact mirror image. As she padded down the hall, she considered changing her sitting room into a nursery for the baby, but the idea had little appeal. All the mint-green paint in the world couldn't make the space as sweetly serene as the nursery at Drake's house.

The door to Courtney's suite stood half-open when Annelise reached the end of the hall. She knocked anyway, calling her stepmother's name for a third time. Again, there was no answer, so she poked her head inside and glanced around.

"Hey, Courtney. It's me." She stepped into the room and raised her voice in case the woman was tucked away in her dressing room. "I'm back."

Still nothing.

Apparently, her stepmother was out, which was odd this time of day. Courtney wasn't exactly an early riser. Annelise figured she must have had ranching business to attend to, so she turned to head to her own suite for a bit before work. She'd have to try and catch her later.

But something strange and out of place caught her gaze just before she turned around. A cardboard box stuck halfway out from beneath Courtney's bed on the other side of the room. Beside it was a can that almost looked like…

Lighter fluid?

Annelise went still.

That was odd. Was Courtney planning on burning something? Her stomach churned at the thought of her stepmother destroying her father's things. He'd only been gone a year, and Annelise knew a lot of his personal effects were still tucked away in every corner of the mansion—his papers, his clothes, things that still carried his scent, even after all this time.

She couldn't bear the thought of Courtney burning Daddy's favorite cowboy hat or the barn jacket that always had his favorite cherry-scented pipe tobacco stashed in the left pocket. Annelise wanted to keep those things. She'd planned on passing the Stetson down to her child someday. Surely Courtney would ask before she got rid of something so personal. The woman was cold, but she wasn't capable of doing something so heartless.

Was she?

Annelise needed to check that box before Courtney came back and burned its contents. She hated to snoop, but this was important. And the way the box looked as if it had been hidden under the bed gave her a really bad feeling. Something wasn't right. Most Texas ranches used burn barrels on occasion, but the state had strict laws about that sort of thing. And Annelise couldn't remember Wellington Ranch ever burning things from the main house.

She cast a glance over her shoulder before crossing the huge room and tugging the box the rest of the way out from under the bed. She'd been right about the lighter fluid. The can felt full, and a book of matches sat next to it, almost like Courtney was ready to set the thing ablaze *inside* the house.

The suite had its own fireplace, so it wasn't completely out of the realm of possibility. But what could she possibly want to burn?

Annelise peered inside the box, but the contents were covered with a dark blanket or some sort of sleeping bag. She pushed it aside, and at first, relief speared through her because she didn't see anything that looked familiar. Definitely not Daddy's hat. The only things she spotted were a pair of glasses she'd never seen Courtney wear before and something furry.

She set the glasses aside to inspect the fur, but as soon as she touched it, she jerked her hand back. It wasn't fur, after all. It almost felt like...*human hair?* Annelise gulped. Then she reached for it again and slowly lifted the mass of hair out of the box.

It was a wig.

Dark...short...

No. A wave of nausea washed over her, and bile rose to the back of her throat. *This can't be what I think it is.*

She tossed the wig back inside the box and scrambled for the blanket that had been placed over everything, but once she unfolded it, she realized it wasn't a throw or a sleeping bag after all. To her absolute horror, it was a long, black, down puffer coat.

Drake's recounting of the way Alice described the woman who'd bribed her into turning over Drake's adoption file rang in her head like a terrible bell.

"If I had to guess, I'd say she was in her thirties.

She had short, dark hair, round glasses, and she wore a big puffy coat."

Courtney was thirty-nine years old, and Annelise had just found an identical disguise to the one the mysterious woman had worn right here in Courtney's bedroom... beside matches and lighter fluid.

She gasped so hard she almost choked. This could only mean one thing: Courtney was the person Drake and Cameron were looking for. How was that possible? Did this also mean she'd been the person who'd lured Drake's secret twin to Emerald Ridge? It had to, didn't it?

Annelise's head was spinning so fast that she could hardly make sense of her thoughts. She felt like she'd stumbled on a box of nefarious puzzle pieces that didn't quite fit together. But then, as she was desperately trying to make it all click, she heard voices somewhere outside.

She froze. Her heart leaped to her throat as she strained to hear. She couldn't let Courtney find her here. If her stepmother was cable of bribery and manipulating the Fortunes, there was no telling what else she might stoop to, especially after she'd been caught red-handed.

Luckily, the voices Annelise heard seemed to be masculine, which most likely meant two of the ranch hands were having a conversation close to the house. Hearing them had been just the wake-up call she needed, though. She needed to get out of here.

Fast.

Hands trembling, she pulled her cell phone from her handbag and snapped a few photos of the box and its contents, along with the matches and lighter fluid. She needed some sort of evidence, and if she took the items, Courtney would know she'd been found out.

The photos were somewhat blurry, but they were the best she could do in a hurry. She shoved her phone back into her purse and tried to leave everything exactly as she'd found it—wig on the bottom, then the glasses, and then the puffer coat folded into a neat square. She nudged the brown cardboard until the box was halfway hidden under the bed again and placed the lighter fluid and the book of matches back beside it.

Then she stood and looked around, praying that she hadn't accidentally left any obvious evidence of her presence behind. Everything seemed in order, so she dashed out of the suite, careful to leave the door ajar, exactly like it had been before.

She held on tight to the staircase railing all the way down. If she tripped and fell in her panic and somehow hurt the baby, she'd never forgive herself. Once she made it to the bottom, she hurried outside, hopped in her car and cranked the engine.

Annelise didn't take a full breath until she'd safely exited the gates of Wellington Ranch without running into Courtney. Then she turned her car in the direction of the only place she knew without a doubt was safe.

Fortune's Gold Ranch.

Chapter Ten

Drake was just about to leave the house to head over to the cattle ranch offices when he heard the screeching of tires in his driveway.

He'd been dragging his feet heading to work in case Annelise changed her mind and came back home. He wasn't sure why. The way they'd left things hadn't exactly been clear, but he didn't like the idea of her going to Wellington Ranch when she'd been so eager to escape the place a week ago.

He couldn't very well stop her from seeing her family, though. And she'd said she was only going there to check on things and see Courtney, not to move back in. But Drake had seen that telltale spark of fear in Annelise's eyes. Whatever was happening between them had her rattled, and all he could do was wait…

What *was* happening between them, anyway? Drake had never fallen so hard and fast for a woman before. He hadn't even told his family she'd moved in with him yet—mainly because he wasn't sure how to do so without spilling the beans about her pregnancy. All he knew for sure was that he wanted—*needed*—Annelise back in his house…his life…his bed. As long as they were together, everything else would fall into place.

Wouldn't it?

Or would he end up feeling like he was on the outside looking in, like he sometimes felt about being adopted? He'd always done his best to ignore those thoughts as a kid, but every so often, his insecurity reared its ugly head. Finding out about Cameron and discovering he was a twin had made those unsettling emotions come rushing right back, and now they were casting a shadow over his relationship with Annelise.

Relationship? His gut tensed. *Who said anything about a relationship? She's having another man's baby, you idiot.*

Drake could love that child, regardless of who the father was. He knew better than anyone that there was more to being a family than genetics. But he wasn't so sure about Annelise's heart. Was she truly over Brad? If he came back, could she really resist the urge to build a family with her baby's birth father?

The screeching tire sound pulled him abruptly out of those troubling thoughts. There must be some kind of trouble on the ranch again—more missing horses or cattle. When was the vandalism going to stop? It had been going on for months already.

He rushed outside, fully expecting to find Vivienne in the truck she used for work as the forewoman of the family's cattle operation. Or possibly Micah, since he was the CEO, although he spent most of his time in an office instead of on the ground like Vivienne did. Whatever had happened, it must be bad if no one had taken the time to pick up the phone and had chosen to speed right over here instead.

His heart dropped all the way to his boots when his gaze landed on Annelise. Her car was parked at an odd angle in the drive, and in her haste, she hadn't pushed the driver's side door all the way shut behind her. The vehicle's security system chimed an alert about the door—*beep, beep, beep.* But the most alarming part of the entire scene was Annelise's expression.

Every drop of color had drained from her face. Her eyes looked almost haunted as she ran toward him.

"Drake! Thank goodness you're still here."

Please let the baby be okay. Drake sent up a silent prayer as she landed squarely in his arms and clung so tightly to him that she knocked the wind out of him. Something was very definitely wrong. *Not the baby... anything but that.*

"I'm here, sweetheart," he said, running a hand over the back of her head. Her hair was like silk against his fingertips. "It's going to be okay. Just tell me what's happened."

She pulled back to look at him, eyes wild. "You're not going to believe it." Her gaze darted around the area. "I think we should talk about it inside."

It almost seemed like she was worried she'd been followed.

Drake felt the hair on the back of his neck stand on end. "Tell me you're okay first. No one hurt you, did they?"

She shook her head and gulped an inhale. "No, I'm okay. I promise."

"And the baby?" His eyes dropped to her stomach.

She curved a hand around her tiny baby bump. It was still so small that Drake was certain no one had noticed it. Their little secret. "The baby is fine. I didn't mean to frighten you. It's just…it's *crazy*."

"Come on." He took a relieved breath, but the way she was shaking still had him on high alert. He pressed a kiss to the top of her head and grabbed hold of her hand. Squeezed it tight. "Let's go inside."

Drake shut her car door real quick and then ushered her inside. As soon as the front door clicked shut behind them, she spun to face him.

"Drake, I know who bribed the woman at the diner to get your adoption file." She swallowed hard.

It was the absolute last thing he'd expected her to say. For a second, the words didn't even make sense. The mental gymnastics it required to switch gears so suddenly took a beat or two.

He'd thought she'd been headed to Wellington Ranch. She hadn't had time to go anyplace else afterward. How could she have discovered anything about whoever had been meddling in his life on a quick trip to her family's mansion?

Unless…

A cold chill crept into Drake's bones.

"And?" he prompted. "Who was it?"

But he knew the name before she even said it. He just didn't want to believe it.

Annelise's pretty face crumpled. "It was Courtney."

"Courtney," Drake repeated. His voice was eerily calm. *Too* calm. Annelise couldn't understand why he didn't seem more surprised. "As in, Courtney Wellington."

"Yes. Courtney, my stepmother." Annelise pressed a hand to her stomach. She thought she'd felt a flutter... maybe even a kick? It was too early for that, though. At least, she thought it was, unless her baby was going to be a soccer phenom. Clearly *anything* was possible if her stepmother was a criminal mastermind. "Why don't you seem surprised?"

Annelise certainly was.

Although the more she thought about it, the more believable it seemed. She'd never completely trusted the woman, and as evidenced by her spectacular failure of a love life, Annelise trusted everyone. It was her fatal flaw.

Here it was again, biting her in the backside.

"I think I'm still wrapping my head around it." Drake's gaze flitted toward the stuffed armchairs by the window. The *coffee chairs*, as Annelise had come to think of them. "Can we sit down and start from the beginning?"

She nodded and wrapped her arms around herself. "Yes. Yes, of course."

Everything was about to change, wasn't it? How could it not?

"Please try and catch your breath. You're here now, and you're safe. That's the most important thing." Drake gave her elbow a squeeze, and she went to sit down while he poured two mugs of coffee—decaf for her and fully loaded for him. He was going to need it once she showed him the pictures she'd taken.

She dug around in her handbag for her phone and clutched it tight until he came back with their drinks. Then she took a deep breath and told him everything that happened, from arriving at the Wellington mansion and finding the house empty, to discovering the disguise, to her mad dash back to his house. Throughout it all, Drake just listened and didn't interrupt once, but Annelise could see the tension in the lines around his eyes.

She hated herself a little for it. In her head, she knew she wasn't responsible for Courtney's actions. But her heart still carried the shame of being such a bad judge of character when it came to Brad. And now this thing with her stepmom...somehow, it felt even worse.

"Here." She handed him the phone once she'd finished recounting all the details. "I took a picture of everything before I put it back exactly like I found it."

Drake enlarged the photo, gaze spanning every detail. "I hate to say it, but you're right. This doesn't look good for Courtney. She had to be the one who paid to get her hands on my adoption file."

"But why, though? That's the part I don't understand. What interest could she possibly have in your past?" Annelise shook her head.

Drake looked out the window and frowned at the pastoral scene. The blades of a windmill turned against the backdrop of the sweeping blue sky. Beneath the grazing cows' feet, the grass glittered so green that it almost hurt to look at it. "What if it's not just my past she's interested in? What if it's my whole family?"

Annelise bit her lip. "You think Courtney wants to harm the Fortunes?"

His gaze turned back to her, and his blue eyes were as sharp as cut diamonds. "The way I see it, there's really no reason for her to bring my twin here and completely disrupt my life unless I'm just one piece of a larger puzzle. What if she's behind everything else—not only looking for information about my adoption to find something that would cause my family trouble, but the sabotage, the thefts and the vandalism, too. All of it?"

A chill ran up and down Annelise's spine. "And she's been hitting her own ranch to deflect suspicion from herself."

"Fortune's Gold Ranch is her biggest competitor. She's trying to cause enough chaos to take us down," he said. "That's the only motivation that makes sense."

He was right. Annelise hated to admit it, but he'd just hit the nail on the head.

Her mind whirled as she sipped her coffee. All the strange things that had been happening in Emerald Ridge were starting to add up. "I bet Courtney stole the Gift of Fortune invitation from the main house the night she invited herself to dinner with your aunt Shelley and cousin Poppy back in January. Didn't you say that's where you keep the invitations since all the family members review the online applications?"

Drake nodded. "We have some there and at the ranch office. Those are the only two places Rafe and I keep them."

If their suspicions were true, Courtney was a fraud... and a liar...and a thief. She'd probably even hired people to help with her dirty work, like the men who'd robbed the Fortune barn and stolen the saddles. She'd always made Annelise uncomfortable, but she'd thought their strained relationship just stemmed from family drama. She'd never thought Courtney was right for her father or that she'd loved him as much as Daddy had loved her. At times, Annelise even wondered if she'd only married him to get her hands on the Wellington Ranch.

But she'd never, ever suspected her stepmother was capable of such cruelty.

"I feel like I should've seen this coming, Drake. I feel awful." Annelise's bottom lip began to quiver. She'd misjudged someone, yet again. And this time, she hadn't been the only one who'd gotten hurt. Drake was a wonderful man, and Courtney hadn't just harmed him. She'd targeted his entire family. Even their horses and cows had suffered. "My stepmother is the closest thing to family that I have left, and I'm horrified that she did this to you."

Drake turned tender eyes on her. "Please don't blame yourself. This isn't your doing, it's Courtney's."

"I know, but—"

"No buts." He shook his head. "Also—and this is important, so listen up, sweetheart—Courtney Wellington is not your family. Your family is made up of the people who love you and hold you dear. That's *not* Courtney. There's a reason you didn't feel comfortable sharing a house with her, and now we know why. But you *do* have a family. You have Jax, and you have your baby. They're your family."

He paused, and just the look on his face was enough to make her heart squeeze tight.

"You've got me too," he said.

Drake was her friend, and he might even want to be her family someday…all she had to do was let him.

Why did that seem so impossible, especially after

what they suspected Courtney had done? Annelise could've stopped her if she hadn't been so blind to what was going on around her. How had her father ever fallen for that woman?

Annelise felt sick.

The same way you fell for Brad.

Poor Daddy. Jax was always saying he had his faults and that he wasn't as perfect as Annelise made him out to be. He'd tried to put a fist through a wall the night their mother died from cancer. Then, after Mom passed away, he'd placed all his trust into someone who'd taken advantage of his vulnerability. Even his vast fortune hadn't been enough for her. She still wanted more, and her greed was destroying everything in its wake.

Annelise was almost glad her father wasn't around anymore to see it. If the heart attack hadn't killed him, this would've shattered him beyond all repair.

"Drake, I...we..." What to say? Annelise didn't know where they could possibly go from here. She wanted him so much, and she knew he already cared about her baby almost as much as she did, but...

She sat up straighter. Something about the word *baby* had just slipped another piece of the puzzle into place.

"Drake," she said again, only this time with an urgency building dead in the center of her chest. "The night Courtney was at the house for dinner—the night we think she stole the Gift of Fortune invitation—that was the same night Baby Joey was left on the porch."

Annelise and Drake stared at each other.

Courtney *was* there that night. Could she have seen the mother leave the baby on the doorstep?

And then another thought occurred to her, another blow to her heart.

All this time, had Courtney known who Baby Joey's parents were and why they'd tried to pass him off as a Fortune?

Chapter Eleven

Drake scrubbed a hand over his face and stood, pacing back and forth in front of the sitting area. Something told him Annelise wasn't going to like what he was about to say, but he didn't have much of a choice.

Courtney Wellington had clearly been responsible for at least some of the recent trouble that had hit the Fortunes, and all signs pointed to a much more far-reaching and disturbing picture. Drake's siblings and cousins had been affected. They had a right to know what Annelise had found at the Wellington mansion.

"I need to loop my family in on this," Drake said.

"I understand." Annelise nodded, then stood and grabbed her purse. "I'll go so you can talk to them. This is the kind of conversation you'll want to have with everyone in person, and I'm sure no one wants me here for that."

"Wrong." He lifted the strap of her handbag from her shoulder and placed it back down in her chair. "Why would I want you to leave? You're the one who cracked the case. Without you, we'd still be completely in the dark."

"True, but Courtney is my stepmother. Won't that

make it weird?" Annelise's pillowy bottom lip slipped between her teeth.

Drake wanted to kiss her right then and there, but now wasn't the time. They still had so much to unpack about Courtney and what, exactly, she'd done to the Fortunes. He hated to consider she might have something to do with the baby left on the doorstep, but if she did, at least they might finally get some answers about Baby Joey.

"I thought we'd just covered this. Courtney isn't your responsibility. Remember?" He tipped her chin upward so her gaze locked with his. Then he gave her a quick, gentle peck on her cheek, right near the corner of her mouth, because he just couldn't help himself and she looked like she could use it. "Besides, I know my family. They're going to be nothing but grateful. You're amazing. I already know it, and now they will too."

That seemed to do the trick, because her lips curved into a smile for the first time since she'd come home from the Wellington Ranch. The tense set of her shoulders relaxed ever so slightly. "How are we going to explain the fact that I've been living here?"

"We're adults. We don't need to explain anything." He winked at her and reached for his phone.

"Somehow, I think your siblings and cousins are still going to have questions," Annelise said. She gave him a playful poke in his ribs as he banged out an urgent group text.

He pressed Send and then looked up from his screen. "It's done. And don't worry. You're one of us now."

It felt like it, anyway, even if it wasn't true in the technical sense. At some point, they needed to have a conversation and figure out what they meant to each other.

First things first, though. They needed to figure out how to prove Courtney's involvement in the ranch sabotage and whatever else she'd been up to before she realized they were on to her. If she was already preparing to burn her disguise, she must've known she was flirting with disaster. It was only a matter of time until she was discovered.

Drake's sister, Vivienne, was the first to respond to his text on the group chat, as well as the first to arrive at his house. Cameron turned up minutes later, and then the rest of the Fortunes descended in a flurry of rapid-fire questions. He did his best to usher them into the living room and get everyone seated, but it was like herding cats.

"I'm not sure what's going on, but whatever it is, I think it's great that you included Cameron in this emergency family meeting," Vivienne said, gaze flicking toward Drake's twin, who was chatting with his cousin Shane on the edge of the crowd.

"This affects him, too." Drake placed his hands loosely on his hips. "I've had a lot of distractions the past week or so, and I haven't gotten to spend as much time with him as I would've liked. He seems great. I hope he's been settling in okay."

"Don't worry about him. He's fine. We've all been rolling out the Welcome Wagon. He's probably enjoyed whatever time he's had to himself. You know how we can be sometimes." His sister scrunched her face. "Just a teensy bit overwhelming."

Drake laughed under his breath. He'd been on the receiving end of his family's hospitality plenty of times. They meant well, but they could indeed be overbearing on occasion. "Thank you for making him feel at home."

"Speaking of making people feel at home." Vivienne cleared her throat and cast a purposeful glance at Annelise sitting beside Poppy on the sofa opposite the windows.

Drake followed her gaze just in time to see Poppy hand Baby Joey to Annelise. Of course his cousin had brought the little tyke with her. Drake rarely saw Poppy without Joey, even at the Fortune's Gold Ranch Spa where she worked as the director.

Annelise's entire face lit up as she gathered the baby in her arms, and then she and Poppy laughed in unison as they realized Joey still had a fistful of Poppy's long blond hair in one of his pudgy little hands. Poppy pried his fist open and smoothed her hair over her shoulder, safely out of reach. Joey laughed like it was all a game. He was such a good-natured baby. Everyone said so.

Drake's heart jerked in his chest. He wanted answers for Joey as much as he wanted them for his family. He'd been a baby just like that once—separated from his birth family and all alone in the world. Drake didn't want that little boy to have to wait thirty-one years to discover who he was or where he'd come from, like Drake had.

He took a tense inhale and then immediately relaxed as his eyes met Annelise's over the baby's head. Her grin lit up the whole room. He suddenly couldn't wait to see her with her own baby in her arms...couldn't wait to possibly be the one to drive her and her child home from the hospital. To hang a mobile over the crib in the mint-green room. To get up in the middle of the night and rock the baby back to sleep.

Just thinking about those things made his throat clog.

"I've seen an awful lot of Annelise Wellington on the ranch lately. It seems you have too." Vivienne gave him a shoulder bump, forcing his attention back to her. "We've all noticed her car in your driveway overnight. Is she living here?"

"Yes," Drake said. "And no, we're not going to discuss it."

Yet...

He wasn't even sure where things with Annelise were headed yet. Once he knew, he'd be happy to let his family in on it.

"Fair." Vivienne nodded. "She looks awfully content here in your house with a baby in her lap, though. And it's pretty obvious you can't keep your eyes off of her."

Drake slid his narrowed gaze toward his sister.

She shrugged and bit back a smile. "Just saying."

"Be nice to her, okay? She's a little nervous about this family meeting," he said.

Vivienne's smile faded. "That sounds awfully ominous. Why would she be nervous?"

"You're about to find out." He nodded toward the lone available seat in his living room—an empty couch cushion with Rafe and Micah on either side.

"Fine. Let's get this started. The curiosity is killing me." Vivienne obediently made her way over to sit down.

"Thank you, everyone, for dropping whatever you were doing and heading straight over," Drake said in a tone loud enough to cut through the chatter in the room.

He waited for everyone to quiet down before continuing. "I've got some new information to share about how Cameron happened to receive a Gift of Fortune invitation and find his way to Emerald Ridge. Frankly, I think it's just the tip of the iceberg, so I wanted us all to get together and come up with a plan to sort things out. Before I go into the details, however, I want you all to know that Annelise Wellington is the one who made this discovery. So we have her to thank."

He paused to flash her a quick wink.

Baby Joey babbled as she bounced him on her knees, and Annelise nodded at his acknowledgment, while the other Fortunes shot her curious glances. Her cheeks went pink, but otherwise, she seemed to be holding up just fine.

"Earlier this morning, Annelise found evidence indicating that Courtney Wellington bribed an employee of the now-defunct adoption agency where Cameron and I were adopted in order to get her hands on my birth records and adoption file," Drake announced.

A collective gasp went up around the room.

Drake went on to tell the rest of the story in detail, including their theory that Courtney had been responsible for the vandalism at local ranches—including her own, as a way to avoid suspicion—and her possible involvement in the confusion surrounding the identity of Baby Joey's mother. When he finished, the other Fortunes were all on the edge of their seats.

"This is big." Micah blew out a breath. "*Really* big."

Shane sighed. "Finally, we just might be getting somewhere with this investigation."

"Thanks to Annelise." Poppy turned to Annelise sitting beside her and gave her knee a pat. "We're all so grateful. Stumbling on that box in your stepmother's room must've been terrifying. I'm so glad you made it out of there without being seen."

So was Drake. If Courtney had come home and found Annelise with her things, there was no telling what would've happened. He couldn't even bring himself to consider how Courtney might have reacted.

She's safe. She's home.

"I'm happy to help." Annelise glanced around the room at Drake's family members. "Seriously, if there's anything else I can do, I will. I can even go back and look around again if we think Courtney might be hiding more physical evidence…"

Over his dead body. No way was he going to let Annelise put herself in danger. There had to be a better way.

"For what it's worth, I agree with both of you." Rafe's gaze darted between Drake and Annelise. "What you've discovered today clearly points to Courtney being behind *everything*."

Vivienne held up a hand. "Same."

"What about Joey, though?" Poppy ran a hand over the baby's wispy hair while he cooed in Annelise's lap. "I just don't see the connection between Courtney and his birth mother. It's the missing piece of the puzzle."

"Poppy is right." Cameron's brow furrowed. Drake was glad he felt comfortable enough to contribute to the conversation. "We need to somehow identify the baby's mother. Once we do, everything will hopefully become crystal clear."

Cameron's gaze slid toward Drake, and it didn't take

any secret twin voodoo to know why his brother had the same worries about Joey's parentage as he did. Neither one of them wanted that little boy to be blindsided later in life, like they had been.

"His mother must have a connection to Emerald Ridge. It's the easiest explanation for how she might've gotten mixed up with Courtney Wellington. Someone has to know something, whether they realize it or not," Vivienne said, and questions shone from her expression as she glanced from one Fortune to the next.

She was grasping at straws, desperate for somebody to remember some tiny forgotten detail that might be a clue. Drake knew, because he'd been doing the same thing for months already. They all had.

"I just thought of something," Annelise said, and every head in the room turned toward her. Her eyes lit up, kindling a spark of hope deep in Drake's chest. They really needed another lead right now. "There's an old-time cowboy on Wellington Ranch named Rufus. He's worked there forever. He's got to be in his seventies by now, but he still works as a ranch hand and has since I was just a little girl. Daddy promised him he'd always have a job for as long as the ranch exists." She took a breath before saying, "Rufus always knows everything that's going on at the property. Maybe I can talk to him and ask if he saw anything around the time Baby Joey turned up on the doorstep five months ago—if he ever saw Courtney meeting with a pregnant woman or anything."

Rafe glanced at Drake. "It's worth a shot, bro."

"I agree. Talking to the old-timer could be promising," Vivienne said.

Promising or not, it was the only plan anyone had come up with.

"I'm in." Drake nodded. "Let's do it. I'll go with you, Annelise."

That last part was nonnegotiable. He couldn't let her go back to Wellington Ranch alone—not while Courtney was still a loose cannon.

Still, he half expected her to argue with him. Annelise had a mind of her own, and she'd already done just about as much to solve this mystery by herself as all the Fortunes combined over the past five months.

"How does first thing in the morning sound?" she asked, and Drake breathed a little easier.

"It sounds like a plan."

As soon as the family meeting ended, Annelise was swarmed by Fortunes, all eager to thank her for sharing what she'd discovered at the Wellington mansion. Drake had been right—she'd been worried for nothing. No one seemed to blame her for her stepmother's alleged misdeeds in the slightest. In fact, a few people even seemed to go out of their way to make her feel welcome at Fortune's Gold Ranch.

"Let me give you a hug," Vivienne said as she wrapped her arms around Annelise. "It's great to see you. I love that you're here, and I know my brother thinks so highly of you. It's good to see him so content like this."

"Oh." Annelise tucked a lock of her hair behind her ear, surprised that Drake's sister seemed to assume they were a couple. "I...we..."

What was she supposed to say?

I'm just staying here while I'm pregnant with another man's baby and my stepmother is tormenting your entire family. But don't worry—it's all totally platonic, except for the part where Drake and I slept together last night. Also, I might be in love with him.

"Cat got your tongue?" Vivienne gave her a knowing grin. "Don't worry. I'm not going to pry, but I can tell Drake cares about you. A lot. He just seems different somehow."

"Maybe it's because he recently found out he has a secret twin," Annelise countered. As much as she wanted to believe she was the reason for any newfound happiness that Vivienne could see in her brother, she just wasn't convinced. She felt like she'd done nothing but drag drama to his doorstep since the day she'd moved in.

Vivienne's eyebrows arched as she aimed a glance at her brother across the room, in deep conversation with Cameron and Rafe. "He doesn't go longer than ten seconds without looking at you."

Right on cue, Drake's gaze darted to Annelise, and he gave her a look that warmed her all the way down to her toes before turning his attention back to his twin and his cousin.

"Told ya," his sister said with a smirk.

"What are we talking about?" Poppy asked as she returned from changing Joey's diaper with the baby propped on her hip.

Vivienne answered before Annelise could get a word in. "Drake and Annelise."

Poppy's face split into a grin. "I knew there was something going on there. He can't stop staring."

"That's exactly what I just told her." Vivienne nudged Annelise with her elbow.

Her face felt like it might burst into flames. "I'm afraid things between Drake and me are...complicated."

Understatement of the century. Her hand flew to cradle her belly before she could stop it.

If Poppy and Vivienne noticed, they were both polite enough to pretend they hadn't.

"Complicated doesn't mean impossible. Sometimes it just means special," Vivienne said. Then she gave Annelise another quick hug before dashing back to work.

"She's right, you know." Poppy ran a soothing hand over Joey's back. "And let me just add that you really have a way with babies. You're a natural."

Her grin widened, and then she too made her way outside with the rest of the cousins.

Maybe the pregnancy wasn't going to stay secret for much longer, after all. Perhaps that was a good thing? Annelise was finding it harder and harder to keep the news to herself. The future didn't seem quite as uncertain as it had even a few days ago. Living here with Drake had gone a long way in making her believe that it was all going to be okay, even without the baby's birth father in the picture.

She thought about the big stuffed panda in her bedroom...the rocking chair and the matching bassinet... and happiness bloomed inside her.

Maybe even better than okay.

She straightened up the sofa cushions and carried empty coffee cups and water glasses to the kitchen while Drake finished saying goodbye to everyone. When he came back inside and shut the front door behind him, it seemed as if the rest of the Fortunes had taken all the oxygen with them when they'd left. How was it that a house this size could feel so small when it was just the two of them?

"I think that went well, don't you?" Drake said, dragging a hand through his hair.

He looked incredibly tired all of a sudden, and Annelise couldn't help but blame herself for at least part of his exhaustion. Finding out about Courtney and trying to figure out where to go from here had no doubt been mentally and emotionally draining, but they hadn't exactly gotten much rest the night before. And once he'd woken up and found out she'd gone back to her own bed, he probably hadn't slept a wink.

Annelise didn't want to talk about Courtney anymore. What was there left to say, anyway?

"Drake, I'm really sorry about the way we left things this morning," she said. She'd replayed their conversation a million times in her head throughout the day, and it made her feel worse every time.

"It's okay," he said.

But it wasn't okay—not really. She wished she could wave a magic wand and fix everything, but every time she felt herself wanting to let go, the more things seemed to spiral out of control.

"Why are you going so above and beyond to help me, Drake?" she asked quietly.

"I…" His mouth tipped into a frown as if he, too, wondered the same thing. "I'm not sure I can explain it. I just know that I want you in my life, Annelise—you *and* the baby. Nothing can change that."

She shook her head. "I'm honestly not sure I'm worth all the trouble."

"Please don't say that," he said, and the earnestness in his tone nearly killed her. "Look, I know things are moving fast between us. I don't fully understand it myself. All I can say is that I've never felt this way about anyone before. For some reason, when I'm around you, my walls come tumbling down."

Annelise knew the feeling all too well.

"Can't we just see where this goes?" he asked.

Annelise wanted nothing more than to take him at his word and say yes. Most of all, she wanted to spend the night in his bed again. She missed the way he'd touched her, like she was the most beautiful girl in the world. Why was it so hard to believe that his feelings for her were real?

Maybe Vivienne and Poppy were right. They probably knew Drake better than anyone else did.

"Complicated doesn't mean impossible. Sometimes it just means special."

Annelise wanted to hang onto those words so badly that it hurt.

"I'm trying. You mean so much to me too," she said around the lump that had sprung to her throat. "I just can't seem to get past my lack of trust. I thought maybe I could, and now this thing with Courtney. I—"

He walked toward her and shushed her with a tender kiss to her lips. "I told you I'm not going anywhere. We've got all the time in the world."

Did they, though? In a matter of months, Annelise was going to give birth. And they were already in a race against time to catch her stepmom before she did something that might damage the Fortunes beyond all repair.

Then he kissed her again—this time with a hunger that told her Drake wasn't quite as patient as he let on. He felt it too, didn't he? The tick-tick-tick of the clock.

"I want you to stay here tonight, though. Please don't go back to Wellington Ranch alone," Drake murmured as he pulled away and pressed his lips to her temple. The seriousness of his words made her mouth go dry.

She shook her head. "I won't."

Annelise never wanted to be alone with Courtney again, thank you very much.

"Tomorrow, we'll head over there to find Rufus and see what we can find out." Drake smiled down at her, and longing wound its way through her. "Together."

"Together," she echoed.

Wouldn't it be nice if someday she'd feel capable of adding *forever* to the end of that sentiment? Right now, the words just wouldn't come, no matter how much she wished they would.

Chapter Twelve

The following morning, Annelise drove Drake to Wellington Ranch in her car. His Porsche didn't exactly fly under the radar, and they'd decided it was probably for the best not to broadcast the fact that a Fortune was on the premises. No one would raise an eyebrow at her presence on the ranch. She doubted if anyone who worked on the range had even realized she'd moved out.

"Since Rufus has been with us for so long, he's got his own cabin. It's near the bunkhouse," Annelise said as she passed the driveway for the mansion and headed toward the section of the property where the working cattle operation was located.

Drake nodded. "Great. Let's start there."

He pulled the brim of his Stetson down as the car wound its way past the barn, a paddock surrounded by a white fence where horses lifted their heads to watch them pass, and continued beyond the cattle feeding area where a line of cows pushed against a metal fence, eager for their morning grain.

"I really don't think we need to worry about Courtney catching a glimpse of you way out here. She doesn't stray far from the mansion." Annelise rolled her eyes. "I'm not even sure she owns shoes appropriate for the range."

Drake laughed quietly. At least they both still had a sense of humor, even though they were on enemy territory.

She couldn't believe she felt so detached from her childhood home, but it wasn't the same place where she and Jax had grown up—especially not now that she suspected what Courtney had been up to for the past five months. She couldn't imagine living here again, even if they somehow proved Courtney had broken the law and got her arrested.

Then what? Was Annelise supposed to move back into the mansion all by herself? She couldn't bear the thought of doing so. Courtney's presence had tainted her memories of growing up there. She wasn't sure she'd be able to stand sleeping under that roof ever again. Besides, she'd built something with Drake...something that was beginning to feel more like home with each passing day.

"There it is." Annelise pointed at the single-story ranch-style building coming up on the left. "Rufus's cabin is right over there."

She passed the bunkhouse and pulled the car into the small dirt lot full of trucks and a few ATVs directly behind it.

Drake peered through the windshield at the modest cabin. A lone chair sat on the small front porch, and a pair of denim overalls and a few white T-shirts were hung on a nearby clothesline.

"Ready?" Annelise asked, pulse skittering.

"As ready as I'll ever be. Let's hope this old-timer can give us some answers," Drake said.

He climbed out of the car and jogged over to open her door before she had a chance to exit the vehicle.

She stepped out of the car, and despite the tension thrumming through her, she couldn't help grinning up at him. His charm caught her so off guard sometimes, and that was quickly becoming one of the things she liked best about him. "I have the most overwhelming urge to lift that Stetson from your head and put it down on mine." She tilted her head. "What do you think that means, cowboy?"

His blue eyes sparkled beneath the hat's gray felt brim. "Pretty sure it means you're flirting with me."

A warm, fuzzy feeling came over her. It felt good to do something as fun and normal as flirting. Everything had been so high-stakes lately. Being around Drake felt like an escape, even here in this place that had once felt like heaven on earth and now just made Annelise sad and nostalgic for simpler times.

"You think?" she asked, eyeballing the hat again.

She didn't dare touch it. Just having this hot, sexy cattle rancher accompanying her put this entire investigation at risk. If Courtney had help with her scheme and the wrong person saw them together, all bets would be off. Any sort of public display of affection was strictly off-limits.

Drake leaned closer, nearly backing her up against the car door. His breath tickled her ear. "It's a well-known fact that when a woman wants to steal your hat, she's got her heart set on something else."

She twirled a lock of her hair around her finger. "You sound awfully sure of yourself."

"You know what else I'm sure about?" he asked, eyes hungry enough to devour her.

Annelise would never get over the electricity that constantly bounced between them. If she weren't so attracted to him, her life would be so much simpler. So much *safer*. She'd been hurt before by men who'd never had this kind of effect on her. This felt dangerous.

"Tell me," she said with her heart in her throat.

Drake's eyes narrowed on the horizon where three quarter horses chased each other along the fence line, dark tails streaming straight behind them. He seemed to be weighing his next words as the ground shook with the thunder of hoofbeats.

Then he turned back to her with determination glittering in his cornflower-blue eyes. "After all this is over, I'm taking you on an actual date. Maybe that feels like we're doing things in reverse order, but I think it's important. You deserve a proper courtship, Annelise."

Her knees went instantly wobbly, and she was suddenly grateful for the support of the vehicle behind her. "You want to court me?"

It was such an old-fashioned word...an old-fashioned *concept*, considering the intensity of the feelings that had been swirling around them for days already. How had it only been a little more than a week since she'd moved into his house when it already felt so much like home?

But that was Drake. Annelise had learned a lot about him during their time together, and she knew he valued things like family, chivalry and doing the right thing.

What could be more honorable than announcing his intentions to court her, even after she'd already given herself to him so completely?

"Yes, ma'am. I do." A grin tugged at the corner of his mouth as he backed away. "Now, let's go solve a mystery so we don't have to wait much longer."

Okay, then.

Annelise smoothed down the front of her pencil skirt and tried to calm the pounding of her heart as she fell into step beside him. She needed a second after that exchange to remind herself why they were here. But then Rufus stepped out of the front door of his cabin, and everything came rushing back in full force.

"Miss Annelise." The elderly man nodded at her. Then his gaze flicked toward Drake. "Sir."

She had no idea if he recognized Drake as a Fortune, and thought it best not to mention it for now, just in case. "Hello, Rufus. Please just call me Annelise. We've known each other forever. There's certainly no need for such formality."

Rufus's eyebrows rose, and he crossed his arms over his faded denim overalls. "Mrs. Wellington might have other ideas."

Annelise fought back an eye roll. Of course Courtney would make the ranch hands address her that way—even someone who'd worked for the family as long as Rufus had.

"Well, Courtney's not here right now, is she?" Annelise countered.

Rufus's mouth twitched like he was trying not to smile. "What can I do for you, Miss Annelise?"

He'd refused to drop the *Miss*, but at least she'd

seemed to establish some rapport with him. "We were wondering if you could help us with something. It's regarding Courtney, actually."

Rufus nodded, wariness creeping into the lines that crisscrossed his weathered face.

"It's nothing big," Annelise added. If he thought he might get in trouble with the big boss, he might never talk. Although from what she remembered of Rufus, that really wasn't his style. He'd always been a bit of a gossip.

"It doesn't have anything to do with the ranch," Drake added.

"Right." She nodded. "We're trying to find someone. Did you happen to notice Courtney meeting with a pregnant woman a while back?"

"This would've been around five months or so ago," Drake said.

Rufus's forehead furrowed as he considered their question. "I'm afraid not. Try as I might, I can't recall a time I ever saw Mrs. Wellington talking to Opal."

Annelise's gaze flew toward Drake. The way his eyes flashed told her he was thinking the exact same thing as she was.

Who's Opal?

Annelise shook her head. "Rufus, I'm not sure who that is."

"Sure you do." The old man hooked his thumbs around the buckles on the bib of his overalls and rocked back and forth on his heels. "Opal—the poor pregnant gal."

"Still not ringing a bell, I'm afraid," Annelise said, trying her best to keep her tone even. This sounded promising, though. Surely it wasn't just a coincidence...

"She's one of the ranch hands out here. New around these parts, which is probably why you don't know who she is. She's real young." Rufus cleared his throat. "I'm pretty sure she was expecting when she got here, but no one knew. Come winter, it looked like she was trying to hide a pregnancy under big, baggy clothes. I noticed, though. Can't say if anyone else did. There was definitely a bun in that oven."

"I see." Drake nodded. Annelise couldn't understand how he sounded so calm when her pulse was going a mile a minute. Could this Opal person be Baby Joey's mother? If she was trying to hide her pregnancy, it seemed like there might be a chance she was.

But what had happened to her baby? Had the girl ever given birth? Surely she had if she'd been showing last winter.

"Rufus, do you know if Opal ever had the baby?" Drake asked.

The older man shrugged. "Can't say for certain, but it sure seems that way. One day, back in late January, she was all the sudden swimming in those big, baggy clothes. I wondered what happened, but I didn't mention it to anyone. I mind my own business." Rufus gave Annelise a sideways glance. "That's one of the reasons your daddy kept me on for so long. I'm loyal like that."

"Yes, you are, and you've been a huge help," Annelise said. Now they just needed to track the young woman down.

"We really appreciate your assistance. Do you know where we might find Opal?" Drake held up his hands. "We promise not to mention you."

Rufus nodded. "Much obliged, sir. She's out yonder

on the range someplace, probably mending the fence along the back acre."

He pointed off in the distance, past the cattle barn and the grain troughs.

"We'll go take a look. Thank you again, Rufus." Annelise felt giddy with this discovery, but she tried to tamp down her excitement. The ranch hand had never seen Courtney speaking with Opal, and they couldn't be certain the girl was Baby Joey's mother.

But she might be…

And that was enough for now, because according to the Fortunes, it was probably the closest anyone had come to identifying the abandoned infant's mother.

"Let's hope this isn't a false lead, like Jennifer Johnson," Drake said under his breath as they walked back toward the car.

Rufus was still standing on his porch, watching Drake and Annelise. Drake could feel the elderly man's eyes on them, and he would've bet his entire net worth that minding his business wasn't as high up on Rufus's list of priorities as he'd indicated.

So far, the old-timer's curiosity appeared to be working to their advantage. But they needed to act quick before Courtney got wind of the fact that Annelise had been asking questions. If anyone on the ranch had recognized Drake as the cowboy who'd accompanied her on her fact-finding mission, there was no telling how her stepmother might react.

"We need to move on this fast," Drake said after they were both buckled back into their seat belts.

"Agreed." Annelise nodded and backed out of the

small lot behind the bunkhouse. "Do you think Opal really might be Joey's mother?"

"It sounds like she might. If what Rufus said is correct, the young woman obviously didn't want anyone to know she was expecting. That might mean she was desperate enough to leave her baby on someone's doorstep." Thinking about that one-day-old child left out in the cold set Drake's teeth on edge.

What kind of desperation led someone to do such a thing? And if the young ranch hand on Wellington Ranch was in fact the baby's mother, how and why had she tried to pass the baby off as a Fortune?

Money was the obvious answer. She'd probably wanted to give her child a better life. But so much had happened since then, with the false DNA results and Jennifer Johnson's extortion. There was clearly more going on than just a simple case of a young woman who was unprepared to be a mother. Identifying the baby's birth mom might just be the tip of the iceberg, but it was a start.

"I don't see anyone." Annelise shook her head, gaze fixed on the horizon, where a split-rail fence stretched as far as the eye could see.

It looked to be cedar, similar to the fencing at Fortune's Gold Ranch, with galvanized wire mesh as added protection for livestock containment. Nothing much could withstand the weight of a four-hundred-pound animal who liked to rub on fence posts, though. Mending fences was part of ranch life, even when there wasn't a saboteur running around the area, intent on causing as much harm as possible.

"There." Drake sat up straighter as the vehicle made

its way down a hill and a slight figure became visible next to a small tractor.

"I bet that's her." Annelise pressed down harder on the accelerator. "Wow, she looks really young."

Even from a few yards away, as she pulled over and parked alongside the fence line, Drake could tell the girl was just a teenager. Eighteen years old, at most. He wondered if she'd even finished high school or if her education had been derailed by her pregnancy.

"We're going to need to tread lightly here." Annelise sighed as she shifted the car into Park and glanced at Opal in the rearview mirror. "I already feel sorry for her. She's just a kid."

Drake nodded. "Agree. Let's start slow and see how it goes."

They stepped out of the car, and the girl held up a hand. "Howdy."

Before either of them could say anything in return, her gaze drifted toward Drake, and her brown eyes widened. The poor teenager froze like a deer in headlights while her straight, dark hair whipped in the wind.

Great. A weight settled on his chest. She obviously recognized him as a Fortune.

"Opal, right?" Annelise extended a hand. "Hi, I'm Annelise Wellington."

The girl's own hands were sheathed in work gloves, and she kept them firmly fixed around the hammer she held. She shot a terrified glance at the tractor as if weighing whether or not to jump in the seat and make a run for it.

Annelise drew her hand back and spoke as gently as

if talking to a timid little lamb. "It's okay, Opal. We're just here to chat. You're not in trouble."

The teenager's eyes darted to Drake again, and her chin started to quiver.

"She's right, Opal. We want to talk, that's all." He swallowed and dove right in. "About your baby."

"What baby? I don't know anything about a baby." She shook her head, but the hammer fell from her fingers as her hand moved to cradle her belly as if from muscle memory.

"Someone left a baby boy on the doorstep of my family's home at Fortune's Gold Ranch back in January. All we want to know is how it happened, I promise." Drake offered her a tender smile. "Joey is happy, healthy and safe."

Hearing her son's name did the trick. As soon as it slipped from Drake's lips, Opal's face crumpled.

Annelise reached for the girl and ran a soothing hand over her back. "He's yours, isn't he?"

A sob escaped her as she nodded. "I didn't mean to cause any trouble, I swear. But look at me—I can't take care of a baby. I can barely take care of myself."

She sniffed and then wiped her face with the cuff of her work shirt, which appeared to be at least three sizes too big. The hems of her jeans dragged the ground and were caked with days' if not weeks' worth of rich Texas soil. If Drake had to guess, he'd say she was still wearing some of the baggy clothes she'd used to try and conceal her pregnancy.

Poor kid. His throat closed. "We can help you, just like my family helped Joey. But first, you need to tell us exactly what happened."

Opal took a ragged inhale. "See? This is why I took him to your ranch instead of leaving him at the main house here. Mrs. Wellington isn't nice like the Fortunes are." She glanced over at Annelise and winced. "Sorry, but it's true."

"I know it is. You can trust me, Opal, I promise." Annelise glanced his way and shifted closer to him. "You can trust both of us."

"Talk to us?" Drake said, imploring her with his eyes. They were so closer to getting some answers. So very close… "Please?"

Opal's eyes welled again. Then her tears spilled over, streaming down her face and making her appear even younger than he'd originally thought. She nodded through a shuddering sob.

"F-fine," she said, and then her shoulders slumped, like she'd been carrying the weight of the world on her slender back for all this time and she'd finally decided to let it go. "I'll tell you everything. Just not here…"

Chapter Thirteen

Minutes later, Opal opened the door to a tiny, single-person cabin near the bunkhouse and ushered Annelise and Drake inside.

"Come on in." She waved a hand toward a plaid sofa that sagged in the middle. "Take a seat."

Annelise glanced around and tried to imagine raising a baby in the small space. An unmade twin bed was pushed against the far wall, and other than the sofa, the only other furniture that occupied the cabin was a card table flanked by two rusty folding chairs. There was no room whatsoever for a crib, let alone the other paraphernalia a newborn needed—things like a changing table, diaper pail, bouncy seat. A lump formed in her throat as she sat down, thinking of her own baby, who would be here before she knew it.

"The foreman gave me my own cabin so I wouldn't have to stay in the bunkhouse with the men," Opal said. She folded her arms in front of her, unfolded them, then folded them again. As Annelise's father used to say, the girl seemed as nervous as a cat in a room full of rocking chairs.

Annelise couldn't blame her, really. She'd left her baby on a stranger's doorstep. It couldn't be easy admitting to something like that, whether or not she'd been involved with Courtney's subterfuge.

Drake sat down beside Annelise. "It's nice that you have some privacy."

"Yeah, well…when Mrs. Wellington found out the foreman let me have this place, she blew up at him. That happens a lot—the yelling." Opal fixed her gaze on the floor. "Like I told you, she's not a nice person."

Shame spiraled through Annelise at the thought of Courtney mistreating the staff. What else had she overlooked since Daddy died? She'd been completely wrapped up in grief, and then building AW GlowCare, and then finding out she was pregnant and navigating the breakup with Brad. It's like she'd been in a fog and was just now seeing her stepmother for who she really was.

"Anyway," Opal continued. "I'm from a few towns over, and my parents kicked me out when they found out I was pregnant. My boyfriend didn't want anything to do with a baby, so I came to Emerald Ridge looking for work."

Annelise swallowed. She could certainly relate to a birth father bailing on his responsibility, but at least she'd had a safety net. And a home. And a support system.

And Drake.

Her hand found his, and she squeezed it hard while Opal went on.

"Being a ranch hand includes room and board, so I thought I'd try all the ranches in the area. I came to this one first, and the foreman hired me on the spot. I didn't tell him I was pregnant, obviously. Who's going to hire a pregnant ranch hand? When I really started showing, I got some big, bulky clothes from the lost and found and hid my belly as best I could until the baby came."

"Did someone take you to the hospital?" Annelise asked gently. She couldn't imagine Courtney helping the girl, but it would explain how she might've become involved.

So far, they hadn't heard anything to indicate that her stepmom even knew about Baby Joey. And she *had* to. There was no way this scared teen girl had been tormenting the Fortunes with fake DNA results and texts about the baby being a Fortune. Annelise refused to believe it.

"No, I had him right over there." Opal jerked her head toward the twin bed, and Annelise thought she might be sick. She'd already discussed her birth plan with her doctor, and it included soothing things like fuzzy socks, meditative music, her favorite AW Glow-Care products, and—most importantly—pain management. Lately, she'd been thinking about asking Drake if he might be her birthing coach. Meanwhile, this poor young thing had given birth right here in a nonsterile cabin…all alone. "I left Joey on the Fortunes' doorstep the next day because I wanted him to grow up and have a good life. It wasn't too cold out that night, and I knew someone would find him fast. I couldn't leave him on the porch of the main house here. What if Mrs. Wellington had decided to keep him? Everyone knows the Fortunes are a good family."

Drake nodded. "That's why you pinned the note to

Joey's blanket that said he was a Fortune...and why you sent the text to my aunt that said Garth was his father. Because you wanted him to be raised as a Fortune."

Opal, who'd been pacing back and forth a bit as she told her story, stopped dead in her tracks. "What text? I never sent a message. I don't even have a smartphone."

She tipped her chin toward the old-fashioned landline that hung on the cabin wall just inside the door.

Pricks of unease began to make their way up Annelise's spine. She *knew* it. This girl was little more than a child herself. Opal hadn't been pulling the Fortunes' puppet strings. Someone else had, and Annelise was certain that person was Courtney Wellington.

"I left the note pinned to Joey's blanket because I wanted him to be a Fortune. I wanted him to grow up on that beautiful ranch with all the love in the world. I wanted him to have everything I could never give him." Her eyes went glassy, and she shook her head. "But I didn't send a text message. Garth Fortune is married. I wasn't trying to hurt anyone, I promise. I placed the baby on the doorstep. Then I rang the bell and I ran. End of story."

She paused to chew on her lip. "Mostly."

"Mostly?" Annelise felt her eyes narrow. "It's important that you tell us everything you know, Opal."

"A few months ago, I snuck onto Fortune's Gold Ranch to try and get a peek of my baby. I just wanted to see him and make sure he was okay." Opal's gaze flicked toward Drake. "I saw your cousin Shane there. He was with Joey at the outdoor spa café, and when I saw them together, something inside me just broke. I should've never gone there. Seeing Joey hurts too much, even though I know giving him away was the right thing. Shane turned his back for a second, and I did something really dumb. I grabbed the stroller with Joey inside and rushed off with it."

Beside Annelise, Drake nodded and steepled his fingers. "So that was you."

"It was me, but I knew it was wrong right away. I'd never be able to take care of Joey as well as Poppy and Leo. I wanted him to stay with them. I still do. You have to believe me. It was just a split-second decision that I regretted as soon as I did it. I only wanted to see him again...to hold him, one last time." Opal's eyes misted over again. "As soon as I realized what I'd done, I let go of the stroller and ran off into the woods."

Annelise had heard about the event, which had been described to her as an attempted kidnapping. It sounded more like a momentary lapse of judgment, albeit a serious one.

"That's all, though. I haven't had any more contact with any of the Fortunes." Opal made an X over the breast pocket of her work shirt with her pointer finger. "Cross my heart."

"I believe you." Annelise cast a questioning glance at Drake. His expression told her he believed Opal, too. But there was so much more that little Joey's birth mother didn't know. Maybe if she did, the three of them could put their heads together and figure out if Courtney could've been responsible for the other mysterious events surrounding the baby's appearance at the Fortunes' front door. "I think we need to tell her the rest, don't you?"

Opal's forehead puckered. "The rest? You mean there's *more*, besides the text message?"

Drake nodded. "A lot of strange things have happened. My cousin Poppy took Joey in because she's a certified foster parent. All the Fortune men submitted to DNA testing to find out if the baby was really part of our family. Before the results came back, Poppy received the anonymous text about Garth. Then the DNA results went missing from the lab."

"Wait a minute! I remember Courtney talking about that at the time. She said maybe Garth had been the one behind the missing DNA results because he really *was* the father and was trying to hide it. I can't believe I forgot about that until just now." Annelise sighed. The signs had been pointing right at Courtney all along, and no one had noticed.

A hard knot of muscle flexed in Drake's jaw. "She said the same thing to Poppy."

Opal's head swiveled from Annelise to Drake and back again. "What happened after the DNA results disappeared? Did anyone ever find them?"

"We retested, and none of the men in my family were a match," he told her. "But later, we thought we found Joey's mother because a woman named Jennifer Johnson's DNA was a match. It turned out to be a hoax. Somehow she'd faked a test with Joey's mother's—with *your*—DNA. The only reason she got caught is that my sister swiped a glass that Jennifer had used in the spa and had it tested to confirm the initial results. It proved she was lying and had faked the test." A muscle clenched in Drake's jaw as he finished filling her in. "Jennifer Johnson still claims to know who you are, and she's trying to extort money from my family to give up your identity."

Opal shook her head. "That's impossible. I don't know anyone by that name. How on earth could she get my DNA?"

"From a drinking glass, like the one Vivienne snagged from the spa," Annelise said.

"Or a toothbrush, maybe?" Drake added.

The girl's head shook even harder. "But I don't know her. How could she get those things unless she snuck in here? I keep my cabin locked. The foreman is the only other person with a key."

"Not the *only* other person," Annelise said, and just like the moment she'd found the box containing the disguise in Courtney's bedroom, everything clicked neatly into place.

"Courtney," Drake muttered. "Of course."

"She runs the ranch. She has access to the entire premises. She was also at the Fortune mansion the night you left Joey there, Opal." Annelise's pulse began to pound with such force that it roared in her ears.

"And we know for a fact that Courtney paid someone for documents about my past," Drake added. "Mark my words, it was her."

Opal gasped, and her round face went completely white. "She must've seen me leave Joey on the Fortunes' porch. I had no idea. She never said a word to me about it."

"Courtney could've easily hired Jennifer Johnson to pretend to be Joey's mother to extort money from my family and distract them so the ranch would suffer. She probably found someone whose coloring matched the baby's and then stole something from this cabin to fake the DNA test." Drake looked around the interior of Opal's home. From the dishes piled in the kitchen sink to the hairbrush lying on the nightstand, her DNA was everywhere.

Everything made sense now—all the crazy twists and turns of the past few months were covered with Courtney's fingerprints. She was the only person with both the motive and the opportunity to get away with all of it.

Annelise dropped her head in her hands and concentrated on breathing in and out. They knew what had happened. Now they just needed to prove it. Somehow that seemed far easier said than done. The only real proof they had of Courtney's involvement in anything illegal were the photos she'd taken of the boxed disguise.

She lifted her gaze to Drake's. He looked every bit as exhausted as she felt. They both had a personal stake in what they'd just learned. Courtney was Annelise's stepmother, and while it was difficult to accept what she'd done, Drake's entire family had been her victims. Knowing someone had gone to such lengths to destroy the people you loved and their livelihood had to be a sobering realization.

"So, where do we go from here?" Annelise asked, and she wasn't entirely sure if she was talking about their investigation or something else...

Later, she told herself. She could figure out how all of this affected what she and Drake had *later*. Their entire relationship thus far had felt like taking two giant steps forward, immediately followed by another step back. Over and over again. And she knew it was her fault.

But this...

This felt like more than just a backward step. Her stepmother was a complete and total monster—a monster who'd tried to tear down everything Drake and his family had built here in Emerald Ridge, including their relationships.

Annelise couldn't think about that right now, though. They'd promised to help Opal if she told them the truth about Baby Joey, and she'd more than held up her end of the bargain.

"I think the first thing we need to do is find Opal another place to stay," Drake said, clearly on the same page as Annelise. He stood and planted his hands loosely on his hips as he offered Opal an apologetic look. "I'm sorry, but I don't think it's safe for you to work here anymore. Once Courtney Wellington realizes she's been found out, there's no telling how she'll react."

"I get it, believe me." The young woman wrapped her arms around herself. "After hearing all this, I don't *want* to work here. Actually, I don't want to be anywhere near Courtney Wellington ever again."

"My family can help you get on your feet someplace new, but in the meantime, we can offer you one of the guest cabins at Fortune's Gold Ranch," Drake said.

Annelise nodded her encouragement. "It's nice there—quiet, peaceful, and even more important, it's safe. You'd like it."

Fortune's Gold Ranch had been just the respite she'd needed. Mostly because of Drake, but the ranch itself was magical. She still couldn't quite imagine her baby growing up anyplace else.

That was bad. She'd become far too attached to Drake—to his heart, to his home, to everything about the man. Which was another thing she'd have to figure out.

Later. The word ushered in a sinking feeling deep in her core. The more Annelise thought about later, the worse it sounded. Was it completely awful that she wished she could stay in the here and now, even with all its accompanying drama?

Opal shook her head, giving the idea of staying with the Fortunes an immediate hard pass. "No. I appreciate the offer, but it would be too hard for me to be so close to Joey. That's where he belongs, not with me. I just can't be around to watch."

"We understand," Annelise said. Surely there was someplace else they could take the girl where she would feel more comfortable.

Drake nodded. "I can book a room at the Emerald Ridge Hotel. We can help you pack up your things and head straight over there. How does that sound?"

"Really nice. Thank you both so much." Opal surveyed the room, no doubt taking stock of all the things she needed to pack up before they left.

There wasn't much, and that was a good thing. Annelise was already getting antsy about Courtney somehow getting wind of their presence on the ranch. She felt protective of the teen and wanted to get her out of here before anything else bad happened. Her stepmother was more unhinged than she ever could've imagined. Annelise shuddered to think what she might do next.

"There's something I need to do first, though." Determination sparked in Opal's eyes. Now that she'd gotten the truth off her chest, she seemed less afraid and more at peace, somehow. Annelise hoped that once she left Emerald Ridge, she could truly start over.

But why was she dragging her feet all of a sudden? They needed to go.

"It's important," Opal insisted.

And the finality in her tone told Annelise that no matter what, exactly, the girl had planned, there would be no stopping her.

Drake busied himself packing up Opal's belongings while the young woman sat down at the card table and began writing something out in longhand. It looked like a letter, but that's about all he knew. He didn't want to look over her shoulder and pry, but at the same time, he couldn't just stand around and wait for her to finish— not when he needed to get her and Annelise off Wellington property before Courtney found out she was about to get exposed.

"I've got all her clothes folded and put away," Annelise said quietly as she handed him a zipped, half-full duffel bag. "I'd like to give her a few of my things to wear, but most of my clothes are still in my closet here at the ranch."

Drake shook his head. No way she was going back there, not even for charitable purposes. "I'm sure Vivienne has some things she can pass on to Opal. Poppy, too."

His heart wrenched at the mention of his cousin. Poppy and Leo loved little Joey so much. Now that his mother had been found, Drake wasn't sure what might happen next. If Opal signed over her rights to her baby, which he suspected she would do, Joey could be put up for permanent adoption. There was no guarantee the state would place him with Poppy and Leo. This new development had the potential to crush Poppy.

Unless...

"Here." Opal handed Drake the letter she'd been working on. "I'm finished."

Drake glanced down at the handwritten page. It looked like a schoolgirl had crafted it in neat, careful lettering.

Dear Poppy and Leo,

I'm writing to you with a heavy heart but also with a sense of relief and hope.

My name is Opal Mackey, and I am the mother of the baby boy you are currently caring for. I can only imagine how surprised and confused the Fortunes must have been when they found Joey at their doorstep. I want to explain why I made that decision and express my sincere thanks for taking such good care of my child.

I'm seventeen, and as much as I wanted to be there for my baby, I came to the painful realization that I cannot provide the life that he deserves. This decision was one of the hardest I've ever had to make, but I believe it was the right one.

When I left Joey in your care, it was because I had heard about what an upstanding family the Fortunes are. I knew my son would be safe and well-cared-for with you. Over time, as I've learned more about your family and seen the way you embraced my child, it's become clear that you have given Joey the stability and love he needs to thrive.

With this letter, I am formally requesting that you consider adopting my baby. I believe that you are the perfect people to give my baby a stable and loving home, and I hope you will take this step to make it official.

I know this is a significant decision and that it will require legal steps and formal proceedings. I am ready to work with you, the authorities, and anyone else involved to ensure that everything is handled smoothly and in the best interests of little Joey. My hope is that we can work together to finalize the adoption and provide my baby with the secure and loving future he deserves.

I appreciate your understanding, compassion, and the care you have already shown my son. I am grateful beyond words for the role you have played in his life these past six months. Please let me know what I need to do next or if there is any other information you need from me. I'm staying at the Emerald Ridge Inn.

Thank you once again for everything. I am hopeful that this letter finds you willing to take on this precious responsibility, and that together, we can give my baby the best possible life.

With deepest gratitude,
Opal Mackey

This was what had been so important for Opal to take care of before she left. Gratitude welled up inside Drake. It was going to mean the world to Poppy. Joey's birth mother had just paved the way for her and Leo to proceed with a formal, private adoption.

In a strange and unexpected way, the note pinned to Joey's blanket had been right all along—the baby really *was* a Fortune.

Chapter Fourteen

After Opal gave Drake her letter expressing her wish for Poppy and Leo to permanently adopt Joey, it only took a matter of minutes to clear out of the little cabin at Wellington Ranch.

Annelise's hands tightened on the steering wheel as the car made its way past the drive to the mansion, eventually spilling on the highway and leaving Wellington property in the rearview. The ranch got smaller and smaller during the short drive to downtown Emerald Ridge, until it disappeared altogether.

Annelise wondered when—if ever—she'd go back there. She supposed she'd have to, eventually, even if only to get the rest of her things. But then what?

She glanced at Opal's reflection in the rearview mirror, struck by how much she and Joey's mother had in common. On the surface, their lives were nothing at all alike. There was a common thread running through their experiences that was undeniable, though. They'd both been hurt and rejected by the fathers of their babies. And now, for wholly different reasons, they'd both been forced to flee from Wellington Ranch. On an emotional level, deep down where a person's sense of security and belonging came from, they were so very much the same.

It was uncanny and more than a little unsettling. Annelise tried to shake the odd feeling as Drake checked Opal into the Emerald Ridge Hotel.

Unfortunately, stepping into the lobby of the luxe, five-star establishment only exacerbated Annelise's sense of unease. Captain's restaurant, the scene of her devastating breakup with Brad, was located on the top floor of this very hotel. She hadn't darkened the door of the Emerald Ridge Hotel since that awful night, when she'd fled after tossing her cranberry juice in her ex's face.

Being back made her chest feel tight, as if she couldn't breathe. She took a deep inhale, but the air smelled sticky-sweet just like it had that night—a nauseating blend of buttercream frosting, red juice and heartbreak.

"Are you okay?" Drake asked, pausing on the way to the registration desk.

Annelise hadn't even realized that she'd stopped moving. She'd come to a dead halt just past the entrance to Emerald Ridge Café, the coffee bar located in the hotel's lobby.

"I—um." She swallowed the bile that rose to the back of her throat. "Fine. I think I'm going to wait outside, though, if you and Opal don't mind. Today has been a lot."

It *had* been a lot. She really hadn't needed such a visceral reminder of one of the worst nights of her life directly on the heels of learning the full extent of Courtney's betrayal.

"Whatever you need." Drake regarded her thoughtfully. Opal was already waiting for him near the registration desk, awkwardly glancing around the opulent lobby. "You're sure everything is all right, though?"

Annelise wasn't sure of anything anymore, but she nodded and forced a smile. "I'm sure."

She waited outside in the shade of the hotel's porte cochere. It only took a matter of minutes for Drake to get a room for Opal, and once he'd joined Annelise outside, he explained that he'd booked her for a week's stay so she had a safe place to live while Poppy and Leo consulted with the Fortune family's attorney and took care of the legalities of adopting Joey.

Annelise could relax again with Drake by her side, and she wasn't sure if that was such a good thing. He meant too much to her. It was obvious now that her entire life had turned upside down. Drake Fortune and the baby she was carrying were the only two things keeping her grounded. Without them, she wasn't sure how she'd manage to keep it together.

"Do you know how bad I've wanted to kiss you all day?" Drake said the instant the front door of his house at Fortune's Gold Ranch closed behind them.

Annelise glanced at him over her shoulder, and he wrapped strong fingers around her wrist, tugging her toward him. She let him reel her in, just like she always did, craving the comfort of his warm embrace...of his strong and steady presence...of the absolute thrill that always lit her up from the inside out whenever his lips touched hers.

"Go ahead and kiss me, then," she whispered, heart beating hard against his firm chest.

He lowered his mouth to hers, and at the first fiery

contact, she nearly wept with relief. He felt so good... *they* felt so good.

Far, far too good to ever think she could trust it.

"Babe?" Drake pulled back a little and eyed her with concern. "Sweetheart, what's wrong?"

"Nothing." She shook her head, even as fear coiled in the pit of her stomach. *Later* had finally come home to roost.

"Then why are you crying?" He lifted his fingertips to her cheek and brushed away the tears she hadn't realized were streaming down her face.

She could've tried to blame her emotional state on pregnancy hormones or pass it off as first-trimester fatigue. But Drake deserved honesty. He'd done so much for her and asked for nothing in return. As difficult as it was to talk about her mixed-up feelings, she couldn't lie. The simple truth was that she was having a hard time moving on from past hurts, mainly because every time she turned around, she discovered another betrayal. Another deception.

The hurts weren't all in the past. Some of them were as fresh as a tender new bruise, practically invisible on the outside. They would soon bloom in devastating color.

"I just can't believe all the hateful things Courtney has done to your family." She swallowed, but it was no use. All the feelings she'd been trying so hard to repress were rising to the surface, reminding her of how many times she'd been wrong about people...of how many times she'd been blindsided and hurt. Would it ever end? "And not just to the Fortunes, but other people in Emerald Ridge too. I can't believe I ever trusted her, even a little bit."

"This is *not* your fault. We talked about this before, remember?" Drake frowned as he searched her gaze. Annelise wasn't sure what he was looking for, but she had a terrible feeling that whatever it was, she couldn't give it to him. And she wanted to…oh how she wanted to. "It doesn't matter what Courtney has done. Nothing else matters but you and me and how we feel about each other. I want you in my life, Annelise—not just for right now and not just until the baby comes."

He was talking about forever, which seemed crazy, given how long she'd been living there. How could such a short time feel like years?

Because they'd been caught up in a whirlwind of intense emotions—not just between them, but because of everything that had been going around them. A secret twin, an evil stepmother, Baby Joey and more. Stressful situations bonded people together, but could those fragile connections really last when they'd been built on such shaky foundations?

Once everything settled down and life went back to normal, would she and Drake feel the same way?

I will, she realized with a lump in her throat. *But will he?*

"My trust is at an all-time low right now," she said. "As is my overall faith in humanity. It's bad, Drake."

A lesser man might've taken her words as a personal insult, but not Drake Fortune. He knew her heart even better than she did.

He cupped her face with both hands, and looked at her with so much love and tenderness in his gaze that she wanted to bottle it and infuse it into her skin care products. If such a thing were possible, she'd be a billionaire. "Come on now, sweetheart. It's me you're talking to. Do you really not trust me?"

Annelise wanted to shake her head no, but she couldn't. It would have been the biggest lie she'd ever told in her life. An undeniable whopper.

"I do trust you, Drake." She felt like crying again, but if she started, she feared she might never stop. She was in love with him and fully incapable of pretending otherwise. "And that's what scares me most of all."

She wasn't sure how he would react to such unflinching honesty, especially since he hadn't given her any reason to believe he might break her heart. But Drake wasn't fazed. He simply took her by the hand, grazed a gentle kiss to her fingers and winked at her.

"Come with me."

"You can look now," Drake murmured, and his breath fanned Annelise's cheek as her eyelashes fluttered open.

They were in one of the barns located on Fortune's Gold Ranch—the one she could see from the big picture windows in Drake's house. He'd promised her a surprise, and at first, she'd thought it was simply the pepperoni pizza they'd picked up at Donatello's on the way home. But then he'd passed the turnoff to his house and kept going, eventually parking alongside the large red building.

"I've never been in a hay loft before. I had no idea they could be this romantic," she said. Her head rested on Drake's shoulder where they laid back on a pile of soft straw. After he'd helped her up a ladder, he'd ordered her to close her eyes while he'd pried open the wooden sliding door on the slanted ceiling, all the while promising her the view of a lifetime. He hadn't been exaggerating. If anything, he'd failed to properly prepare her for the magnificent sight of glittering stars against the velvety night sky.

Drake chuckled, low and deep, and the sound seemed to reach all the way down to her toes. "The stars really are bigger and brighter here in Texas, aren't they?"

He was referencing lines of a song she'd heard since her childhood. Every kid who'd grown up in Texas knew the words by heart. But their meaning hadn't fully sunk in until now.

"It kind of makes you feel sorry for the other fortynine states, doesn't it?" she whispered.

She was only teasing, but as she said it, she realized with unflinching certainty that this was the perfect place to raise a child. Not just her home state, but right here on Fortune's Gold Ranch. She couldn't imagine a more idyllic setting. Every time the outside world felt like it was spinning out of control, Drake brought her back here and she felt hopeful again. It was a little slice of heaven—calm in the midst of an ever-growing storm.

As if he could read her mind, Drake said, "I used to come here a lot when I was a kid. I'd climb up the ladder and just lie here watching the sky turn from blue to pink to amber. Then I'd count the stars as they came out, one by one. It probably sounds crazy, but sometimes I let myself think it was a show just for me."

"That doesn't sound crazy at all," Annelise countered. "Everyone wants to feel connected to the world around them, especially children. Believing that made you feel like you belonged here…like you were a part of things here at the ranch."

He gave her a little nudge with his shoulder. "You're a part of things here too, you know."

Annelise's eyes grew watery. She wanted to believe him so bad that it hurt.

He turned his head just far enough to kiss her cheek. His lips were warm and soft, and as the sweet scent of hay tickled her nose, she thought it might be the most perfect moment she'd ever experienced. Perfect enough that her doubts faded to the background long enough for her to finally take a deep breath. Annelise closed her eyes and burrowed deeper against Drake's shoulder, savoring the sound of crickets chirping and the swish of horse tails in the quiet night. If she could've saved this little slice of time and tucked it between the pages of a book like a pressed flower, she would've done so in a heartbeat.

"Thank you for this." She sniffed as a tear slipped from the corner of her eye. "I needed this reminder that the world is still a lovely place, despite all the pain and heartbreak that sometimes comes with it."

"Anytime, darlin'," Drake said, more tenderly than she'd ever heard him before. "Let me know when you're ready for pizza."

The box sat an arm's length away, untouched thus far.

"I will. I just want to stay like this a little bit longer. Is that okay?" she whispered.

"Whatever your heart desires, ma'am."

What *did* her heart desire?

This, she thought. *This man and this place, now and forever. Not just temporarily.*

If only her head could catch up and stop making things seem so complicated...

Drake woke up the following morning more determined than ever to prove Courtney Wellington's guilt.

He wasn't sure if this single-minded focus was simply a distraction from the fact that Annelise had slept in her own room last night again or if his unconscious mind had somehow seized on the idea that if he could put an end to Courtney's rampage, Annelise might finally feel ready for a new beginning. Or maybe he just wanted to hold the woman accountable for tormenting his family all year long.

Something told him his motivation wasn't quite so linear. His desire to bring Courtney Wellington to justice was most likely fueled by all of those things combined, along with a dash of good old-fashioned anger.

The woman had plotted and conspired to hurt the people he loved, and it was time to make it stop. Luckily, after he and Annelise had come home from the barn, Drake had spent enough time tossing and turning during the wee hours to come up with a plan. Once the idea had crystallized in his mind, he'd finally been able to get some shut-eye. He'd woken up to the pink rays of a blazing sunrise and the sound of hoofbeats as the cowpokes did their regular morning check on the herd.

Back in the barn, the grooms would be mucking out stalls after having turned out the horses. Cattle would be moving from one pasture to another. The rhythm of life on the ranch would move on with its everyday poetry, consistent and true.

As always, Drake took solace in the familiar refrain.

And he'd move heaven and earth to protect this place, if it was the last thing he did.

"I've been thinking," he said as he handed Annelise a mug of decaf. She sat in one of the chairs facing the big picture window, as had become her routine. Drake hated to imagine that chair without her in it some morning, if she decided to leave. He couldn't...not now. Not yet. "Maybe if we go to the hospital, we can track down the lab tech who was responsible for handling the DNA tests on Baby Joey's paternity."

Annelise peered up at him over the rim of her coffee cup. "Didn't the police already question the lab tech? It seems like they would have, especially after the first round of DNA results on the Fortune men disappeared."

"They did." He nodded. "But we've got more information now. Courtney most likely had something to do with those results going missing. And we think she stole Opal's DNA to ensure a fake result on Jennifer Johnson's testing. If she resorted to bribery when it came to getting my adoption records, who's to say she didn't do the same when it came to the lab."

"You think she bribed the lab tech." Annelise's head bobbed in a slow nod. "My goodness, I bet you're right."

"All we need is one person to crack and admit to direct knowledge of her involvement. Once we get a corroborating witness to come forward, her house of cards will start to tumble." Drake angled his head toward Annelise. "Come with me to the hospital?"

"Are you kidding? I wouldn't miss it. We've made such great progress the past few days." She smiled into her mug.

Drake gave her foot a playful nudge with the tip of his cowboy boot. "What's that grin for?"

"I was just thinking." Her eyes sparkled with the promise of a thousand tomorrows. Did she have any idea how beautiful she was when she let her guard down? "We're kind of a great team, aren't we?"

We absolutely are. How about we keep it up, for better or worse?

Drake didn't dare say it.

Instead, he just nodded. "I think you might be right."

They made it to the county hospital in under an hour, just after the morning shift change. As soon as they walked in, Drake recognized the lab tech as the same one who'd been on duty when he'd come in for his initial DNA test, back when all the Fortune men had submitted to testing.

"Mr. Fortune." The lab tech, a thin, wiry man with a pointed chin and chunky, black frame glasses, looked at him askance. Clearly, he'd been caught off guard by Drake's unexpected appearance. "Can I help you with something? If you have orders from a physician for bloodwork, I'm afraid I'm going to have to send you to the third floor. This lab is only for DNA testing and forensics."

Nice try. The guy wasn't getting rid of them that easily.

"I'm not here for bloodwork. I'm here to ask you a few questions," Drake said.

The lab tech adjusted his glasses and glanced at his smartwatch. "I have a very full schedule today and don't really have time—"

Drake held up a hand. "Fine, then. I'll cut to the chase.

We know Courtney Wellington was involved with the DNA errors in the Baby Joey case."

"Um." The tech's eyes went huge, and he stuffed trembling hands in the pockets of his lab coat.

"If she pressured you into anything, it would be better to go ahead and admit it now than get caught later in a lie," Annelise chimed in.

"You should know that we've identified the baby's real mother, and Courtney Wellington had access to her DNA, which was stolen without the mother's consent. She's willing to talk to the police, and when she does, I'm sure the Emerald Ridge PD will be dropping by to pay you a visit." Drake crossed his arms. "Is that what you want?"

"No police." The lab tech shook his head. Beads of sweat were already gathering on his forehead. "P-please."

Drake waited a second or two for him to say more. When he didn't, he turned toward Annelise with a shrug. "Maybe we should go ahead and call Detective Ebert."

"Good idea." Annelise slipped a hand into her designer bag and pulled out her phone.

"No! I did it, okay? Mrs. Wellington can be quite—" he gulped "—persuasive. She was willing to pay a lot of money, and I have credit card debt, okay? This was a way for me to get out from under it."

"How, exactly?" Drake asked. "What specifically did Courtney pay you to do?"

"She said it would be easy and that I wouldn't be hurting anyone. All I had to do was 'lose' the test results for you and the other Fortunes. That's it." The tech let out a shaky breath. "At first, anyway."

"And then?" he prompted.

"And then, a little while later, she came back and wanted me to use a certain DNA sample that she provided as a match for another person who came in for testing in the Baby Joey case."

"What was the name of the person she wanted matched with the DNA sample she brought in?" Drake asked, but he knew the answer before the lab tech even said it.

"Jennifer Johnson."

Drake and Annelise exchanged a glance. This was it—the exact proof they needed to get her stepmom charged with a crime.

"Look, I'm sorry. I really am." The tech mopped at his forehead with a handkerchief. "But I needed the money…"

As if that was a legitimate excuse for the utter chaos this man's actions had caused.

Drake shook his head. "I'm sorry, too. Because I'm going to see to it that you're fired, and I'm also going to report you to law enforcement."

"N-no." The tech glanced frantically between Drake and Annelise. "You can't do that."

"We can, and we will." Drake nodded at Annelise, still holding her cell phone. "Go ahead and make the call."

She tapped the screen. 9…1…

Before she could dial the last digit, the lab tech bolted past her and ran into the hallway. The phone fell from her hands, landing on the hospital floor with a clatter and skidding across the polished tile.

Drake's heart jumped straight to his throat.

"Annelise! Are you okay?" He grabbed her arms to steady her, but she didn't seem off-balance. In fact, she hadn't teetered a bit on her sky-high heels.

"I'm fine. He startled me, that's all. I wasn't expecting him to take off like that." She glanced over her shoulder in the direction where the slim man had disappeared. "Should we go after him?"

Drake shook his head. "No. He's a hospital employee, and the police have already questioned him once. They'll know where to find him. Besides, do you really think I'm going to let you hotfoot it after a criminal in those shoes?"

He arched a brow at her patent leather stilettos. Only Annelise Wellington would wear heels like that to question a possible crook.

"I could catch him if I tried, you know." She tilted her head. "Like Marilyn Monroe once said, 'Give a girl the right shoes and she can conquer the world.'"

"I have no doubt that Marilyn was correct and you could indeed conquer the world." He placed a gentle hand on her small swell of a baby bump. "But humor me and stay put, okay? You've done enough. We never would've gotten this far if you hadn't found that box in Courtney's bedroom at the ranch. You're the one who set all of this in motion. I think we can leave the actual apprehension up to the police."

Annelise rested one of her hands on top of his so they were both cradling the new life growing inside of her. A slow smile tipped her lips. "You make a convincing argument. Maybe I'll conquer the world another day."

"You don't have to conquer it all on your own," he

rasped, and then immediately wished he could reel the words back in.

She already knew he wanted to be part of her future. If she wanted the same thing, she'd let him know. He was beginning to feel like that same boy who'd snuck into the barn at night to bottle-feed a newborn calf— emotionally invested up to his ears, even though the outcome would most likely be dire.

That calf hadn't made it, and for the first time, he was starting to wonder if he and Annelise wouldn't either. His gut told him she was in love with him, but if growing up on a ranch had taught him anything, it was that love sometimes wasn't enough.

"I knew that guy was bad news the second we walked in here," she said, deftly sidestepping Drake's comment.

"Because he tried to get rid of us so quickly?" He removed his hand from her baby bump, bent to retrieve her phone and handed it to her.

Her fingertips lingered on his as she took it from him, like she wanted an excuse to keep touching him. "No, I could tell just by looking at him. The stress of lying and covering up for Courtney is quite literally written all over his face."

And your feelings for me are written all over yours, Drake thought. A sense of bittersweetness settled in the center of his chest.

"He could use some AW GlowCare serums. If he weren't going to jail and all." Annelise laughed, but it didn't quite reach her eyes. She was slipping away, wasn't she? They'd just heard yet another story about Courtney that had shaken her faith in people. Annelise didn't even have to say it—Drake could see each revelation chipping away at her, one at a time. It must feel like the earth falling away beneath her feet, piece by piece, until there was nowhere safe left to stand.

Stand here...with me.

But then she pulled her hand away from his, tucked her phone back into her handbag and hugged the purse to her chest. A barrier.

"That's exactly where he's going. All the skin care in the world can't save that guy." Drake tried to chuckle, but it stuck in his throat. He swallowed hard. "Should we head over to the police station and tell them what we know?"

Annelise nodded. "Absolutely."

The end was coming for Courtney Wellington, but it just might be coming for them, too.

Chapter Fifteen

The next few hours passed at the speed of light. If Annelise hadn't been sitting down in one of the worn vinyl chairs in the Emerald Ridge Police Department, she would've been dizzy in a way that had nothing to do with being pregnant.

Detective Ebert, the lead investigator on both the Baby Joey case and the ongoing ranch sabotage, listened patiently as she and Drake shared everything they'd uncovered in the past few days. He agreed that Courtney appeared to be the mastermind behind everything, but as both Annelise and Drake knew, the trick was going to be collecting enough evidence to put her behind bars for more than just a few days.

To do that, they'd need a search warrant, which would hopefully yield enough physical evidence to tie her to some of the crimes. The photos Annelise had taken in Courtney's bedroom weren't enough. They'd need more in order for a judge to approve a search of the Wellington premises, as the detective had been explaining before the rotary phone on his desk rang, interrupting their conversation.

"Oh, really? That's good news." Detective Ebert leaned back in his chair and flashed Annelise and Drake a silent thumbs-up as he listened to the caller, whose voice she could hear in a tinny rush of words, all the way from her seat on the opposite side of the desk.

Beside her, Drake vibrated with tension. He'd been on edge ever since they left the hospital. They both had. Annelise wanted this whole ordeal to be over. She felt like she'd been living in a weird state of limbo or a bad dream that kept going on and on, and she couldn't wake up, no matter how many times Drake tried to kiss her back to life. She was Sleeping Beauty, and she kept falling under...

The detective hung up the phone, and the rattle of the receiver settling back into its cradle snapped Annelise back to the present moment, even though she still felt like she was experiencing it through a fog of disbelief.

"Good news." Detective Ebert grasped the surface of his cluttered desk with both hands. "While we've been speaking, the emergency search warrant came through. Officers are already on the scene, as is Courtney Wellington. The moment they find anything, they'll take her into immediate custody."

Annelise blinked. *"Really?"*

It seemed far too good to be true, but what were the chances that her stepmom hadn't already disposed of every last bit of evidence?

The detective nodded. "That will only happen if we locate physical evidence tying her to any of her suspected crimes—the bribery, the thefts, the vandalism. We've already got a corroborating witness, though, and that helps. Plus, I'll obviously need to speak to Alice at the diner, along with…" He consulted the information he'd been scribbling into his note pad since Annelise and Drake's arrival. "Opal Mackey. You said she's currently staying at the Emerald Ridge Hotel?"

"Yes." Drake frowned. "Backing up just a second, you mentioned a corroborating witness? Who is that, exactly? I didn't think Annelise and I counted since we didn't directly witness Courtney committing any crimes."

"You don't. I was talking about the lab tech you confronted this morning. While the three of us have been talking, hospital security tracked the guy down right there on the premises." The detective huffed out a laugh. "They found him hiding in a broom closet just down the hall from the lab. The instant our officers arrived, he started talking. That's how they were able to secure the search warrant."

At long last, a bit of the tension appeared to lift off Drake's shoulders. Annelise reached for his hand and covered it with hers. When he glanced over at her, his eyes were shiny.

The detective stood. "Now that I've taken down all your information, I'm going to head over to Wellington Ranch and see what I can do to help out there. We need to find something—the more, the better. Barring a confession, physical evidence and statements from additional witnesses are the only way we're going to see justice here."

"Thank you, Detective." Drake nodded.

"Yes, thank you," Annelise said.

"I'll leave you two to show yourselves out." Detective Ebert came around from behind his desk and grabbed a hand radio on his way out. He paused before walking out the door. "I'll be in touch."

Then he was gone, leaving Annelise and Drake alone to absorb this new information.

Right that second, police officers were going through her childhood home, searching for evidence of Courtney's misdeeds. It was strange to think about them combing through the rooms where she'd grown up... the barn where she'd first learned to ride a pony.

"Do you think they'll find anything?" Drake asked quietly.

"I sure hope so." Annelise's gaze slid toward him. "Because I can't see Courtney confessing to anything. Can you?"

His face fell. "Not for a second. That woman is a pathological liar. I've never known anyone so duplicitous."

Annelise wanted to agree, but then she thought of Brad. He'd been duplicitous too, just in a different way. He hadn't broken any laws. Only her heart.

Detective Ebert's phone rang again, making her jump.

"Let's get out of here." Drake unfolded himself from the other office chair and offered his hand to help her up. "I should probably get all the cousins together at Fortune's Gold Ranch and let them know what's going on."

Annelise stood too. "Good idea."

Maybe it would be nice to wait for information about the search with Drake's siblings and cousins. If anything, it would be a nice distraction from the guilt that had settled in the pit of her stomach.

She couldn't keep stringing Drake along like this.

She needed to make a decision—either she trusted him with her heart or she didn't. It wasn't fair to keep taking from him without giving anything in return.

Annelise had never been that sort of person. Her brother, Jax, wouldn't believe it if he could see her now. The sweet, naive girl that she'd once been had finally cracked. She'd always looked for the best in people, but now that she'd taken off her rose-colored glasses, she couldn't see the forest for the trees.

Seconds after the detective's phone stopped ringing, it started up again. Then a loud siren wailed in the distance, growing louder as it came closer...

"Let's go," Drake said, holding on to her elbow as they made their way out of Detective Ebert's small office, toward the entrance to the police station.

Officers were scurrying about the building, grabbing hats, buckling holsters and rushing for the exit. Outside, the blare of the siren came to an abrupt stop. Flashing red-and-blue lights swept through the lobby.

Then they walked outside, and Annelise couldn't believe what she saw.

"How *dare* you!?" Courtney screeched as a uniformed officer helped her out of the back seat of a squad car. "Get your hands off me. Don't you know who I am?"

Annelise gasped and her hand flew to her mouth as Drake pulled her closer and wrapped an arm around her shoulders.

"Ma'am, you've been placed under arrest. We've already read you your rights and explained the charges. It's time to get inside the station," the officer said with exaggerated calm.

Courtney whipped her head in his direction, eyes filled with fury. "I'm Courtney Wellington. You can't arrest me. I run this town. Get these handcuffs off of me right now."

The second officer in the squad car exited the driver's side and came around to flank Courtney. "As we've explained twice already, ma'am, we can't do that. You're in police custody now, and if you're not careful, you're going to rack up another charge. Resisting arrest is no joke."

Annelise watched, stunned, as her stepmother, who never left the house without being perfectly coifed and dressed to the nines, dropped to the ground and proceeded to kick and scream like a toddler on the asphalt.

"Let me go! I told you—I'm a Wellington. I pay your salary." She tried to gesture to the other officers who'd come outside—ostensibly for backup since she was causing such a scene—but with her wrists handcuffed behind her, the best she could do was thrash about. "All of your salaries!"

"Is this really happening?" Annelise whispered. The nightmare she'd been living in had just taken a surreal turn. It felt more like a fever dream.

"It certainly seems that way," Drake said under his breath.

"I can do whatever I want. Of course I bribed the guy at the lab. The woman from the adoption agency, too. I sent the texts about the baby on the doorstep and stole the Gift of Fortune invitation right out from under everyone's noses. The ranch sabotage—that was me, too. I did it all, and you bumbling idiots never had any idea."

Drake coughed. "Until now."

Annelise grabbed his arm and finally tore her gaze away from her obviously deeply disturbed stepmother. "Was that just—"

"A *confession*?" A smile creased his handsome face, and Annelise felt the first stirrings of wakefulness deep in her heart. It was time to open her eyes. "Sure sounded like one to me."

He pressed his lips to the top of her head, and joy rose up from the very bottom of her soul. She was finished with her rose-colored glasses. Finally she could see just a little bit of light.

So this is what it's like to be kissed awake after a long, dark night.

"Me too."

Drake shot off another urgent group text to his siblings and cousins. By the time he and Annelise pulled up to the house, his driveway looked like a tailgate party— Fortunes and their vehicles everywhere. The only thing missing were refreshments...and maybe a nearby football game.

"Drake!" Vivienne wasted no time running to the Porsche as soon as he found space for it. "Annelise, hi. What's going on?"

Poppy wasn't far behind, and as usual, little Joey was perched on her hip. He clutched a fistful of brightly colored plastic teething keys and seemed unfazed by the small army of people that surrounded him. This kid was going to make a great Fortune.

"I caught everyone up on the situation with Opal already." Poppy winced. "I hope that's okay."

"Of course it is." Drake gave her a one-armed hug.

She and Leo had been scheduled to meet with Opal at their attorney's office earlier this morning to get the paperwork for the private adoption started. Poppy had asked Drake to hold off on telling the others that they'd found Joey's mother until she had an assurance from the lawyer that the adoption wouldn't be a problem and that Opal hadn't backtracked on what she'd written in the letter.

Drake understood. Poppy and Leo had waited months to officially make Joey their son.

"Any news about Baby Joey is yours to share, Poppy. Not mine," he said.

Last night, after they'd returned from the hayloft, he could tell Annelise was still a bit on edge so he urged her to take a bubble bath with the calming AW Glow-Care products she loved so much—the ones that made her skin smell like sun-ripened strawberries and pink heirloom roses. He worried about her pregnancy. She'd been under constant stress for weeks. It couldn't be good for the baby.

He blamed himself for that. Staying with him was supposed to help her cope, not make things worse. He should've stuck to his vow and kept things between them platonic. But he'd gone and done exactly the opposite, and then she'd gotten dragged into his family drama.

If only he'd known that Courtney was the culprit...

Would he truly have done anything differently?

Drake knew better than to pretend he would've. Knowing what he did now, he wouldn't have changed a thing that day at Coffee Connection. Given the chance for a do-over, he'd walk right up to Annelise again and offer to buy her a slice of lemon loaf. He'd stay and talk with her until she had to leave for her doctor's appointment. He'd still paint his walls soothing mint green after she'd moved in, and he'd still take Annelise to bed when she asked him to.

And then they would've ended up in the same place all over again. Drake didn't even know where that was anymore.

While Annelise had been in her bubble bath last night, he'd headed over to his cousin's house to deliver Opal's letter to Poppy and Leo in person and get them caught up on the circumstances surrounding the baby's birth. Never in his life had he seen someone crumple beneath the weight of overwhelming joy the way Poppy had when she'd read Opal's letter.

That was the kind of joy he wanted for Annelise—happiness so pure that it took her breath away.

"We're still just ecstatic," Poppy said as she fell in step beside him, heading for the door to the house. His other family members waited on the porch, except for Vivienne, who'd latched on to Annelise and appeared to be pumping her for information. Of course his head-strong sister couldn't wait five minutes for the family meeting to commence. "I hoped for this all along—prayed for it, even—and it's finally happened. It just goes to show, never lose faith when your heart tells you something is meant to be, Drake. Things have a way of working out when you least expect them to."

"Then again, sometimes they don't," he murmured.

Poppy cradled the back of Joey's head in her hand as she aimed a questioning glance at Drake. "What did you say?"

"Nothing. It's just been a long day, and Annelise and I have a lot to share."

"But it's all good news, right?" Poppy's forehead puckered.

Great. He'd made her worry, when there was nothing whatsoever for her to be concerned about. Not anymore.

"I promise it's all good news, Pop Tart," he said, using one of Rafe and Shane's favorite childhood nicknames for her. Rafe told him a while back that Poppy hated being called Pop Tart back in the day but found it endearing now that they were all older.

"Aw, Drake. You always know how to say the perfect thing to make me feel better." She grinned, and just like that, the worried furrow in her brow disappeared.

But she trained her gaze on him all the way to the porch. And just before they joined the rest of the group, she tugged on his shirtsleeve and pulled him to a stop. "If all the news is good, why do you look so sad?"

Because not everything works out, no matter how very much you might want it to.

Were he and Annelise meant to be?

A year from now, would she be the woman grinning up at him with a baby propped on her hip?

Drake didn't know, but he hoped so. Oh, how he hoped.

Chapter Sixteen

Annelise's second Fortune family meeting was a lot more jovial and boisterous than the first one had been.

After all the cousins, plus Cameron, filed into Drake's house, they migrated to the same seats they'd occupied just a few days prior when they'd met to discuss the disguise that Annelise had found in Courtney's bedroom. Drake's family members all wore the same concerned expressions they had then, anxious to hear why he'd called another emergency gathering.

Just wait, Annelise thought.

"Thanks for coming over again so soon," Drake said as he paused to make eye contact with each person, which made Annelise go a little misty-eyed.

He cared so much about his family. Over the past week, she'd seen him work tirelessly to protect their ranch. Not just the physical property, but the heart of Fortune's Gold Ranch—the people who lived, loved and worked here.

Annelise had been there too, right alongside him. But she'd been so devastated to learn Courtney had been involved that she hadn't realized the deeper meaning of what she'd been witnessing. Drake had been fighting for his family, but he'd also been showing Annelise everything she needed to know about him.

He was strong, yet tender. He was loyal and true. He'd welcomed Cameron into the Fortunes fold with open arms. The care and compassion he'd shown Opal brought tears to her eyes every time she thought about it.

In the beginning, Annelise had been bowled over by Drake's kindness toward her, but it hadn't been until they'd thrown themselves into the investigation that she'd seen the honorable way he moved about the world...the empathy he carried in his heart.

If that kind of man couldn't be trusted, then no one could.

"Drake, go ahead and spit it out. The suspense is killing us," Rafe called out.

"Sorry, I think I'm just a little emotional right now because this whole ordeal is finally over." Drake scrubbed his face.

"Wait." Vivienne sat up straight beside Annelise. "Did you just say 'over'?"

Drake's lips tipped into a crooked grin. "I sure did, sis. That's why I sent the group text. Courtney Wellington is in police custody, and from the looks of things, she's not going to be free for a long, long time."

For a stunned second, no one made a sound. Then Rafe let out a loud whoop, and the Fortune cousins all started talking at once.

"But how?"

"What happened?"

"How do we know she didn't have an accomplice? Shouldn't we still be concerned about that?"

Drake told them what happened at the hospital earlier in the day when they'd gone to confront the lab tech, followed by their trip to the police station. He explained how the guy's statement had paved the way for an emergency search warrant, which had led to the discovery of a treasure trove of stolen goods hidden in the barn at Wellington Ranch.

"They found our stolen horses right there in the stables," Drake said.

Shane's face flooded with relief. "They found Birdy?" He'd been beside himself with worry over his beloved mare that went missing a few months ago.

Drake nodded. "Yep, they sure did. The police located the missing saddles, too. They were in the same barn as the horses, hidden beneath a pile of saddle pads and blankets. The Emerald Ridge PD is taking an inventory of everything tonight, snapping photos and documenting the stolen items. They've got to match the items up with the original police reports, which might take a few days." He exhaled a long, deep breath, his mind still reeling from all the evidence that had come to light during the search. "She'd been targeting all the local ranches, not just ours. We should get everything back in due time, but Detective Ebert said we could bring a horse trailer around tomorrow and pick up the mare."

As promised, the detective had called with an update after he'd arrived on the scene. Drake's cell phone rang just as they were leaving the police station, and he'd given them the whole laundry list of things the officers had found on Wellington property. As soon as they'd located the first few pieces of stolen goods, they'd arrested Courtney on the spot.

The rest was history, of course, because Annelise and Drake had witnessed Courtney's outburst with their own eyes.

"So Courtney was behind *everything*." Vivienne shook her head. "How can we be sure the charges will stick? She can probably afford the best criminal attorneys out there."

Drake's and Annelise's eyes met, and he gave her a tiny nod, prompting her to announce the biggest reveal of all.

She took a deep breath. "Courtney confessed."

The news was met with a round of gasps.

Annelise felt a grin tug at her lips at the memory of Courtney screaming her laundry list of crimes at the entire police department. It had been a scene straight out of a trashy reality television series. "Y'all missed quite a show. It was nothing short of a spectacle."

I'll stick to my comfort shows, thank you very much. The Gilmore Girls *are more my speed.*

Shortly after the two of them recounted the details of Courtney's outrageous confession, the mood turned celebratory. Leo showed up with a case of wine from his family's winery, Leonetti Vineyards. Rafe's wife, Heidi, arrived minutes later with the twins in tow. Soon, Naomi, Jacinta and Jonathan descended on the house, and all the Fortunes were paired off.

Except for Drake and Annelise.

Someone fired up the grill while Rafe made a quick trip to the restaurant at the guest ranch and returned carrying enough seasoned steaks to feed an army. It was a full-fledged party, with Fortunes spilling onto the back patio and deck. The children splayed themselves onto the hammocks like starfish, and when Cameron lit the fire pit, Shane's son, Brady, asked if they could make s'mores.

"I think I spied some chocolate bars and jumbo marshmallows in Drake's pantry the other day." Annelise ruffled the little boy's hair. "I'll go grab them and see if I can track down some graham crackers while I'm at it."

She slipped inside the house and made her way to the kitchen. Deep in the back corner of the pantry, she found all the fixings for s'mores, including skewers for roasting the marshmallows. Annelise supposed if you lived in a house on a scenic ranch and that house came equipped with an elegant fire pit, keeping such things on hand was mandatory.

She gathered the necessary items and then promptly dropped the skewers when she exited the pantry and ran smack into Poppy and Vivienne. The metal rods hit the tile floor in a clatter, like the world's noisiest game of pick-up sticks.

"Oh, no. We're so sorry." Vivienne bent to gather the wayward skewers.

"We didn't mean to startle you. I promise." Poppy bit her lip. "We actually came in here to check on you. It's been so crazy that we haven't had a chance to catch you alone until now. And hey, nice shoes."

Both women dropped their gazes to the bunny slippers Annelise had changed into. She'd kicked off her stilettos after the party had gotten into full swing, and they were the only flats she'd brought with her from the Wellington mansion when she'd packed for her "temporary" getaway.

Vivienne clutched the skewers to her chest. "Seri-

ously, though, are you okay? Courtney is your stepmother. This can't be easy for you. We shouldn't be
celebrating like this. My brothers and cousins are idiots."

Annelise laughed. "No, they're not. They're actually
kind of wonderful."

One Fortune in particular.

"Everyone is relieved, myself included. This has been
a difficult time for all of us, not just me." Annelise's
smile went wobbly. Her stepmother had tormented their
family for months, and *they* were apologizing to *her.*
"I'm glad you all feel like celebrating, and I'm especially happy to be included."

"Of course you're included. After everything we've
been through together, you're like family now," Poppy
said.

Like family.

The qualifier tugged at Annelise's heart. What might
it be like to be a real member of Drake's family?

"You're sure you're okay, though?" Vivienne studied
her, and somehow Annelise had a feeling that Drake's
sister could see straight through to her soul—to all the
hidden parts she'd been doing her best to ignore since
Drake had come into her life. The wants, the hopes,
the dreams.

How would she ever be a good mother if she refused
to let herself believe in her dreams anymore?

Annelise took a shaky inhale as Vivienne's question
about her being okay echoed in her mind.

Just days ago—weeks and months, even—her answer would have been automatic. No, she hadn't been
okay. But things felt different now. She had a baby to

think about, and now that Courtney was locked away, she felt like she could fully focus on the future. Maybe she could even call Jax, finally get her brother to come back to Emerald Ridge.

Brad had pulled the rug out from under her on her birthday, and she'd thought she'd been ready for a new start afterward. But she hadn't...not really. She'd still been clinging to a past life that didn't exist anymore. Old feelings and old memories that no longer served her well. Maybe her life needed to completely burn down to the ground before she could really start anew.

All she knew right now was that she finally felt at peace. She was ready.

"I'm okay," Annelise said. "I promise."

Vivienne nodded. "Good. And for the record, I'm really glad Drake brought you here. You fit in amazingly well."

"Then maybe I should stay a while." Annelise cleared her throat. She couldn't believe she was having this conversation with Drake's sister and cousin while standing in his kitchen with an armful of marshmallows and bunny slippers on her feet.

Poppy winked at her. "Maybe you should."

Annelise's heart felt full to bursting. She liked these women a lot and hoped they could get to know each other better, but right now, there was someone else she needed to talk to. These feelings had been building in her all day with an urgency she couldn't ignore anymore.

"Speaking of Drake, does either of you know where he is? I haven't seen him for a while." Annelise glanced toward the big picture window in the living room. Outside, Rafe and Cameron stood at the grill. The other adults held glasses of wine from bottles with the Leonetti logo, and the kids ran barefoot on the emerald-green lawn. Beyond the dreamy summer tableau, cattle grazed in the distance.

Annelise almost felt like she was looking at a moving painting of the perfect Texas summer evening. The only thing missing was the man she loved. He had to be around here someplace, though.

"I think I saw him head that way a little bit ago." Vivienne tipped her head in the direction of the suite where Annelise had been staying.

That was odd.

Annelise swallowed. "Oh."

"Here, let me take those from you." Poppy plucked the big bag of marshmallows from her arms, along with the chocolate bars and graham crackers. "We'll get the s'mores started. You go find your man."

Her man.

Annelise liked the sound of that an awful lot.

"Thank you." She gave Poppy and Vivienne each a quick hug. "For everything. I mean it."

"Back at you. Don't be long!" Vivienne waved with her free hand as they headed outside.

"We'll save you a s'more, but only if you hurry," Poppy said with a laugh. "I can't make any promises. The Fortunes are a big family."

Big, without a doubt. Boisterous, on occasion. And above all, loyal.

After they'd gone, Annelise stood in the kitchen for a moment, soaking up the silence. Today had been crazy, but ultimately in a good way. And it was about to get even better. She hoped so, at least.

"Drake?" she called out as she padded toward her suite.

There was no answer, and at first, she thought Vivienne had been mistaken. The bedroom was empty, and it looked exactly as it had when Annelise had darted in here earlier for her slippers. But then her gaze snagged on something new that hadn't been there before. Something bold and bright. A crystal vase full of lemon-yellow flowers sat on her nightstand. Their petals had ruffled edges, like fine lace, and bloomed with such bright intensity that it was like looking at sunshine in a bottle.

Happy tears pricked the backs of Annelise's eyes.

"Daylilies," she whispered.

Then her eyes shifted beyond the colorful blossoms to a figure standing in the mint-green nursery, watching her with a heat in his gaze that made her weak in the knees.

"Drake?" She walked toward him on wobbly legs. "Thank you for the beautiful flowers. Where did you manage to find daylilies at the drop of a hat?"

"I have my ways." He shrugged one of his massive shoulders, and in a flash, Annelise could see her head resting against it throughout all of life's most important moments. "Actually, there's a whole garden of them up near the main house. You might not want to tell Darla and Shelley I stole a few."

"Your secret is safe with me." She moved closer, growing more and more breathless with each step. "Is that why you're hiding here in the nursery? Because you've turned into a flower thief?"

He smiled, but there was a sadness in his eyes that tore her up inside.

He doesn't realize, she thought. *He still thinks I don't trust him.*

"I just like to come here sometimes and think about the future," he said, and his eyes dropped to her baby bump. "About that little guy or gal and what it would be like to have them grow up here on the ranch. I hope we can start fresh, sweetheart. I know what you need most right now is time and space, but—"

"Stop." Annelise shook her head and rested her hand on his chest, where she could feel his heartbeat beneath her fingertips, steady and true. "That's not what I need. What I need most right now is you, and I believe you promised me something once all the drama with Courtney was over."

He smiled, and the worry lines around his eyes disappeared, replaced by an expression that made her heart turn over in her chest. "Are you telling me that you might be ready for me to take you on that date I mentioned yesterday?"

Annelise arched a brow at him. "As long as that date involves an altar and a little white wedding chapel, then yes. I'm ready."

His expression radiated pure joy, and he tilted his head. "Are you—"

"Proposing? Yes, I am." Look at her go. She really did feel like she could conquer the world, and she didn't even need her girl boss stilettos to do it. All she needed was the man standing in front of her and the promise of a fresh new tomorrow with him by her side. "I love you, Drake. So, so much. And if you feel the same..."

He stopped her before she could finish. "Oh, sweetheart. I do."

I do...

Why did those words feel like the vow they so often were? Annelise could practically hear the unspoken second part of that promise.

Forever and ever, until death do us part.

She'd never forget this moment as long as she lived. Someday, they could tell their children and grandchildren about it. They were going to be a family...they *were* a family. Starting right now.

Her head spun as she grinned up at him. "I know it's crazy fast, but nothing has ever felt this right before. You're the one. It's as simple as that. The only one for me, and the only one for my—*our*—baby."

His eyes filled, and they somehow looked bluer than ever here in this special room with its soothing mint-green walls.

Annelise rose up on tiptoe and whispered her next words against his lips. If she didn't kiss him soon, she might faint. Pregnancy hormones be damned. The flutter coursing through her was all him. Always was, always would be.

"Drake Fortune, will you marry me?"

Epilogue

One month later...

"Speech! Speech!" Leo Leonetti stood at the far end of the farm table from Annelise and raised his glass.

The crystal flute was filled with sparkling wine—from Leonetti Vineyards, obviously—as were all the other champagne glasses around the table, except Annelise's. She'd officially entered her second trimester, and even though she figured a sip or two wouldn't hurt, especially at her own engagement party, she'd opted to stick to fizzy apple juice.

She still wasn't sure who'd first come up with the idea for this gathering. Like the impromptu celebration after Courtney's arrest, plans for the engagement party had just sort of happened. A few days after Annelise proposed, Drake shared the happy news with his family and then doubled down on the good news by telling them that Annelise was expecting. Everyone had been thrilled and lovingly supportive, which was especially touching since their unconventional courtship had moved with the speed of light.

Make no mistake, it was definitely a courtship. Drake had obviously been serious when he'd insisted that she deserved to be properly courted. Since the day he'd said yes, they'd been on more date nights than she could count. And despite the fact that Darla and Shelley had threatened to hide every pair of gardening shears in the Lone Star State, he kept the crystal vase on Annelise's nightstand filled with fresh-cut daylilies, day after glorious day.

Except her nightstand was located in Drake's room now instead of the bedroom she'd occupied when she'd first moved in. They'd expanded the baby's nursery to take up the entire suite of rooms. Last weekend, Drake had thrown a painting party, and Micah, Rafe, Leo, Cameron, Shane and Jonathan had all pitched in to help transform the entire suite into a mint-green paradise.

Now here they were, at yet another gathering of the Fortune cousins, except there was nothing casual or spontaneous about this one. A lump had formed in Annelise's throat when she and Drake arrived at the guest ranch and spotted the long table out on the lawn, draped with swags of white tulle and clusters of sweet-smelling magnolias. Crystal chandeliers hung overhead from the branches of the live oak trees—six in all. One to represent each couple who'd come together to celebrate the upcoming nuptials: Poppy and Leo, Rafe and Heidi, Micah and Jacinta, Shane and Naomi, Jonathan and Vivienne, and Drake and Annelise.

"Did no one hear me just now?" Leo tapped his champagne flute with a silver fork and glanced around the table. "I said 'speech.' Don't we all want to hear from the one who will be walking down the aisle next weekend?"

All eyes turned toward Drake, beaming as he rose from his chair.

"Not you, bro." Leo grinned and gestured toward Annelise with his glass. "I meant your better half. We've heard enough speeches from you lately. Besides, a little birdie told me that Annelise has something important to say."

Leo winked at her. Everything was happening just as they'd planned, and clearly, Drake was none the wiser.

He aimed a bemused glance at Annelise as he sat back down. "Go right ahead, sweetheart. If you've got something to say, I'm all ears."

Annelise stood and fixed her gaze with his as she lifted her glass in the air.

"I just want to tell everyone here how happy I am to be a part of your family. Drake, I love you more than you'll ever know. We both do—your soon-to-be wife and your—" she swallowed around the lump in her throat "—beautiful daughter."

"Daughter?" Drake's hand flew to his chest, and his mouth dropped open. She'd surprised him, all right. "It's a girl?"

A chorus of cheers went up around the table. Glasses clinked, champagne flowed, and Annelise couldn't seem to stop smiling.

"We're really having a girl?" Drake said as he tugged gently on her arm to pull her down onto his lap.

"We are," she whispered and placed her head on his strong shoulder, just liked she'd dreamed she would in this most precious of moments.

There would be so many more—an entire lifetime full of love and laughter—an eternity spent right here with this man, with these people, as part of a family again. Annelise had found her forever as surely as if she'd struck gold, right here at Fortune's Gold Ranch.

* * * * *